I

TWO HUNDRED THOUSAND FRANCS REWARD!...

"Lupin," I said, "tell me something about yourself."

"Why, what would you have me tell you? Everybody knows my life!" replied Lupin, who lay drowsing on the sofa in my study.

"Nobody knows it!" I protested. "People know from your letters in the newspapers that you were mixed up in this case, that you started that case. But the part which you played in it all, the plain facts of the story, the upshot of the mystery: these are things of which they know nothing."

"Pooh! A heap of uninteresting twaddle!"

"What! Your present of fifty thousand francs to Nicolas Dugrival's wife! Do you call that uninteresting? And what about the way in which you solved the puzzle of the three pictures?"

Lupin laughed:

"Yes, that was a queer puzzle, certainly. I can suggest a title for you if you like: what do you say to *The Sign of the Shadow*?"

"And your successes in society and with the fair sex?" I continued. "The dashing Arsène's love-affairs!... And the clue to your good actions? Those chapters in your life to which you have so often alluded under the names of *The Wedding-ring*, *Shadowed by Death*, and so on!... Why delay these confidences and confessions, my dear Lupin?... Come, do what I ask you!..."

It was at the time when Lupin, though already famous, had not yet fought his biggest battles; the time that preceded the great adventures of *The Hollow Needle* and *813*. He had not yet dreamt of annexing the accumulated treasures of the French Royal House nor of changing the map of Europe under the Kaiser's nose: he contented himself with milder surprises and humbler profits, making his daily effort, doing evil from day to day and doing a little good as well, naturally and for the love of the thing, like a whimsical and compassionate Don Quixote.

He was silent; and I insisted:

"Lupin, I wish you would!"

To my astonishment, he replied:

"Take a sheet of paper, old fellow, and a pencil."

I obeyed with alacrity, delighted at the thought that he at last meant to dictate to me some of those pages which he knows how to clothe with such vigour and fancy, pages which I, unfortunately, am obliged to spoil with tedious explanations and boring developments.

"Are you ready?" he asked.

"Quite."

"Write down, 20, 1, 11, 5, 14, 15."

1

"What?"

"Write it down, I tell you."

He was now sitting up, with his eyes turned to the open window and his fingers rolling a Turkish cigarette. He continued:

"Write down, 21, 14, 14, 5...."

He stopped. Then he went on:

"3, 5, 19, 19..."

And, after a pause:

"5, 18, 25..."

Was he mad? I looked at him hard and, presently, I saw that his eyes were no longer listless, as they had been a little before, but keen and attentive and that they seemed to be watching, somewhere, in space, a sight that apparently captivated them.

Meanwhile, he dictated, with intervals between each number:

"18, 9, 19, 11, 19..."

There was hardly anything to be seen through the window but a patch of blue sky on the right and the front of the building opposite, an old private house, whose shutters were closed as usual. There was nothing particular about all this, no detail that struck me as new among those which I had had before my eyes for years....

"1, 2...."

And suddenly I understood... or rather I thought I understood, for how could I admit that Lupin, a man so essentially levelheaded under his mask of frivolity, could waste his time upon such childish nonsense? What he was counting was the intermittent flashes of a ray of sunlight playing on the dingy front of the opposite house, at the height of the second floor!

"15, 22..." said Lupin.

The flash disappeared for a few seconds and then struck the house again, successively, at regular intervals, and disappeared once more.

I had instinctively counted the flashes and I said, aloud:

"5...."

"Caught the idea? I congratulate you!" he replied, sarcastically.

He went to the window and leant out, as though to discover the exact direction followed by the ray of light. Then he came and lay on the sofa again, saying:

"It's your turn now. Count away!"

The fellow seemed so positive that I did as he told me. Besides, I could not help confessing that there was something rather curious about the ordered frequency of those gleams on the front of the house opposite, those appearances and disappearances, turn and turn about, like so many flash signals.

They obviously came from a house on our side of the street, for the sun was entering my windows slantwise. It was as though someone were alternately opening and shutting a casement, or, more likely, amusing himself by making sunlight flashes with a pocket-mirror.

"It's a child having a game!" I cried, after a moment or two, feeling a little irritated by the trivial occupation that had been thrust upon me.

"Never mind, go on!"

And I counted away.... And I put down rows of figures.... And the sun continued to play in front of me, with mathematical precision.

"Well?" said Lupin, after a longer pause than usual.

"Why, it seems finished.... There has been nothing for some minutes...."

We waited and, as no more light flashed through space, I said, jestingly:

"My idea is that we have been wasting our time. A few figures on paper: a poor result!"

Lupin, without stirring from his sofa, rejoined:

"Oblige me, old chap, by putting in the place of each of those numbers the corresponding letter of the alphabet. Count A as 1, B as 2 and so on. Do you follow me?"

"But it's idiotic!"

"Absolutely idiotic, but we do such a lot of idiotic things in this life.... One more or less, you know!..."

I sat down to this silly work and wrote out the first letters:

"Take no. ..."

I broke off in surprise:

"Words!" I exclaimed. "Two English words meaning...."

"Go on, old chap."

And I went on and the next letters formed two more words, which I separated as they appeared. And, to my great amazement, a complete English sentence lay before my eyes.

"Done?" asked Lupin, after a time.

"Done!... By the way, there are mistakes in the spelling...."

"Never mind those and read it out, please.... Read slowly."

Thereupon I read out the following unfinished communication, which I will set down as it appeared on the paper in front of me:

"Take no unnecessery risks. Above all, avoid atacks, approach ennemy with great prudance and. ..."

I began to laugh:

"And there you are! *Fiat lux!* We're simply dazed with light! But, after all, Lupin, confess that this advice, dribbled out by a kitchen-maid, doesn't help you much!"

Lupin rose, without breaking his contemptuous silence, and took the sheet of paper.

I remembered soon after that, at this moment, I happened to look at the clock. It was eighteen minutes past five.

Lupin was standing with the paper in his hand; and I was able at my ease to watch, on his youthful features, that extraordinary mobility of expression which baffles all observers and constitutes his great strength and his chief safeguard. By what signs can one hope to identify a face which changes at pleasure, even without the help of makeup, and whose every transient expression seems to be the final, definite expression?... By what signs? There was one which I knew well, an invariable sign: Two little crossed wrinkles that marked his forehead whenever he made a powerful effort of concentration. And I saw it at that moment, saw the tiny telltale cross, plainly and deeply scored.

He put down the sheet of paper and muttered:

"Child's play!"

The clock struck half-past five.

"What!" I cried. "Have you succeeded?... In twelve minutes?..."

He took a few steps up and down the room, lit a cigarette and said:

"You might ring up Baron Repstein, if you don't mind, and tell him I shall be with him at ten o'clock this evening."

"Baron Repstein?" I asked. "The husband of the famous baroness?"

"Yes."

"Are you serious?"

"Quite serious."

Feeling absolutely at a loss, but incapable of resisting him, I opened the telephone-directory and unhooked the receiver. But, at that moment, Lupin stopped me with a peremptory gesture and said, with his eyes on the paper, which he had taken up again:

"No, don't say anything.... It's no use letting him know.... There's something more urgent... a queer thing that puzzles me.... Why on earth wasn't the last sentence finished? Why is the sentence...."

He snatched up his hat and stick:

"Let's be off. If I'm not mistaken, this is a business that requires immediate solution; and I don't believe I *am* mistaken."

He put his arm through mine, as we went down the stairs, and said:

"I know what everybody knows. Baron Repstein, the company-promoter and racing-man, whose colt Etna won the Derby and the Grand Prix this year, has been victimized by his wife. The wife, who was well known for her fair hair, her dress and her extravagance, ran away a fortnight ago, taking with her a sum of three million francs, stolen from her husband, and quite a collection of diamonds, pearls and jewellery which the Princesse de Berny had placed in her hands and which she was supposed to buy. For two weeks the police have been pursuing the baroness across France and the continent: an easy job, as she scatters gold and jewels wherever she goes. They think they have her every moment. Two days ago, our champion detective, the egregious Ganimard, arrested a visitor at a big hotel in Belgium, a woman against whom the most positive evidence seemed to be heaped up. On enquiry, the lady turned out to be a notorious chorus-girl called Nelly Darbal. As for the baroness, she has vanished. The baron, on his side, has offered a reward of two hundred thousand francs to whosoever finds his wife. The money is in the hands of a solicitor. Moreover, he has sold his racing-stud, his house on the Boulevard Haussmann and his country-seat of Roquencourt in one lump, so that he may indemnify the Princesse de Berny for her loss."

"And the proceeds of the sale," I added, "are to be paid over at once. The papers say that the princess will have her money tomorrow. Only, frankly, I fail to see the connection between this story, which you have told very well, and the puzzling sentence...."

Lupin did not condescend to reply.

We had been walking down the street in which I live and had passed some four or five houses, when he stepped off the pavement and began to examine a block of flats, not of the latest construction, which looked as if it contained a large number of tenants:

"According to my calculations," he said, "this is where the signals came from, probably from that open window."

"On the third floor?"

"Yes."

4

He went to the portress and asked her:

"Does one of your tenants happen to be acquainted with Baron Repstein?"

"Why, of course!" replied the woman. "We have M. Lavernoux here, such a nice gentleman; he is the baron's secretary and agent. I look after his flat."

"And can we see him?"

"See him?... The poor gentleman is very ill."

"Ill?"

"He's been ill a fortnight... ever since the trouble with the baroness.... He came home the next day with a temperature and took to his bed."

"But he gets up, surely?"

"Ah, that I can't say!"

"How do you mean, you can't say?"

"No, his doctor won't let anyone into his room. He took my key from me."

"Who did?"

"The doctor. He comes and sees to his wants, two or three times a day. He left the house only twenty minutes ago... an old gentleman with a grey beard and spectacles.... Walks quite bent.... But where are you going sir?"

"I'm going up, show me the way," said Lupin, with his foot on the stairs. "It's the third floor, isn't it, on the left?"

"But I mustn't!" moaned the portress, running after him. "Besides, I haven't the key... the doctor...."

They climbed the three flights, one behind the other. On the landing, Lupin took a tool from his pocket and, disregarding the woman's protests, inserted it in the lock. The door yielded almost immediately. We went in.

At the back of a small dark room we saw a streak of light filtering through a door that had been left ajar. Lupin ran across the room and, on reaching the threshold, gave a cry:

"Too late! Oh, hang it all!"

The portress fell on her knees, as though fainting.

I entered the bedroom, in my turn, and saw a man lying half-dressed on the carpet, with his legs drawn up under him, his arms contorted and his face quite white, an emaciated, fleshless face, with the eyes still staring in terror and the mouth twisted into a hideous grin.

"He's dead," said Lupin, after a rapid examination.

"But why?" I exclaimed. "There's not a trace of blood!"

"Yes, yes, there is," replied Lupin, pointing to two or three drops that showed on the chest, through the open shirt. "Look, they must have taken him by the throat with one hand and pricked him to the heart with the other. I say, 'pricked,' because really the wound can't be seen. It suggests a hole made by a very long needle."

He looked on the floor, all round the corpse. There was nothing to attract his attention, except a little pocket-mirror, the little mirror with which M. Lavernoux had amused himself by making the sunbeams dance through space.

But, suddenly, as the portress was breaking into lamentations and calling for help, Lupin flung himself on her and shook her:

"Stop that! ... Listen to me ... you can call out later. ... Listen to me and answer me. It is most important. M. Lavernoux had a friend living in this street, had he not? On the same side, to the right? An intimate friend?"

"Yes."

"A friend whom he used to meet at the café in the evening and with whom he exchanged the illustrated papers?"

"Yes."

"Was the friend an Englishman?"

"Yes."

"What's his name?"

"Mr. Hargrove."

"Where does he live?"

"At No. 92 in this street."

"One word more: had that old doctor been attending him long?"

"No. I did not know him. He came on the evening when M. Lavernoux was taken ill."

Without another word, Lupin dragged me away once more, ran down the stairs and, once in the street, turned to the right, which took us past my flat again. Four doors further, he stopped at No. 92, a small, low-storied house, of which the ground-floor was occupied by the proprietor of a dram-shop, who stood smoking in his doorway, next to the entrance-passage. Lupin asked if Mr. Hargrove was at home.

"Mr. Hargrove went out about half-an-hour ago," said the publican. "He seemed very much excited and took a taxicab, a thing he doesn't often do."

"And you don't know. ..."

"Where he was going? Well, there's no secret about it. He shouted it loud enough! 'Prefecture of Police' is what he said to the driver. ..."

Lupin was himself just hailing a taxi, when he changed his mind; and I heard him mutter:

"What's the good? He's got too much start of us. ..."

He asked if anyone called after Mr. Hargrove had gone.

"Yes, an old gentleman with a grey beard and spectacles. He went up to Mr. Hargrove's, rang the bell, and went away again."

"I am much obliged," said Lupin, touching his hat.

He walked away slowly without speaking to me, wearing a thoughtful air. There was no doubt that the problem struck him as very difficult, and that he saw none too clearly in the darkness through which he seemed to be moving with such certainty.

He himself, for that matter, confessed to me:

"These are cases that require much more intuition than reflection. But this one, I may tell you, is well worth taking pains about."

We had now reached the boulevards. Lupin entered a public reading-room and spent a long time consulting the last fortnight's newspapers. Now and again, he mumbled:

"Yes ... yes ... of course ... it's only a guess, but it explains everything. ... Well, a guess that answers every question is not far from being the truth. ..."

It was now dark. We dined at a little restaurant and I noticed that Lupin's face became gradually more animated. His gestures were more decided. He recovered his spirits, his liveliness. When we left, during the walk which he made me take along the Boulevard

Haussmann, towards Baron Repstein's house, he was the real Lupin of the great occasions, the Lupin who had made up his mind to go in and win.

We slackened our pace just short of the Rue de Courcelles. Baron Repstein lived on the left-hand side, between this street and the Faubourg Saint-Honoré, in a three-storied private house of which we could see the front, decorated with columns and caryatides.

"Stop!" said Lupin, suddenly.

"What is it?"

"Another proof to confirm my supposition...."

"What proof? I see nothing."

"I do.... That's enough...."

He turned up the collar of his coat, lowered the brim of his soft hat and said:

"By Jove, it'll be a stiff fight! Go to bed, my friend. I'll tell you about my expedition tomorrow... if it doesn't cost me my life."

"What are you talking about?"

"Oh, I know what I'm saying! I'm risking a lot. First of all, getting arrested, which isn't much. Next, getting killed, which is worse. But...." He gripped my shoulder. "But there's a third thing I'm risking, which is getting hold of two millions.... And, once I possess a capital of two millions, I'll show people what I can do! Good night, old chap, and, if you never see me again...." He spouted Musset's lines:

"Plant a willow by my grave,

The weeping willow that I love...."

I walked away. Three minutes later—I am continuing the narrative as he told it to me next day—three minutes later, Lupin rang at the door of the Hôtel Repstein.

"Is monsieur le baron at home?"

"Yes," replied the butler, examining the intruder with an air of surprise, "but monsieur le baron does not see people as late as this."

"Does monsieur le baron know of the murder of M. Lavernoux, his land-agent?"

"Certainly."

"Well, please tell monsieur le baron that I have come about the murder and that there is not a moment to lose."

A voice called from above:

"Show the gentleman up, Antoine."

In obedience to this peremptory order, the butler led the way to the first floor. In an open doorway stood a gentleman whom Lupin recognized from his photograph in the papers as Baron Repstein, husband of the famous baroness and owner of Etna, the horse of the year.

He was an exceedingly tall, square-shouldered man. His clean-shaven face wore a pleasant, almost smiling expression, which was not affected by the sadness of his eyes. He was dressed in a well-cut morning-coat, with a tan waistcoat and a dark tie fastened with a pearl pin, the value of which struck Lupin as considerable.

7

He took Lupin into his study, a large, three-windowed room, lined with bookcases, sets of pigeonholes, an American desk and a safe. And he at once asked, with ill-concealed eagerness:

"Do you know anything?"

"Yes, monsieur le baron."

"About the murder of that poor Lavernoux?"

"Yes, monsieur le baron, and about *madame le baronne* also."

"Do you really mean it? Quick, I entreat you...."

He pushed forward a chair. Lupin sat down and began:

"Monsieur le baron, the circumstances are very serious. I will be brief."

"Yes, do, please."

"Well, monsieur le baron, in a few words, it amounts to this: five or six hours ago, Lavernoux, who, for the last fortnight, had been kept in a sort of enforced confinement by his doctor, Lavernoux—how shall I put it?—telegraphed certain revelations by means of signals which were partly taken down by me and which put me on the track of this case. He himself was surprised in the act of making this communication and was murdered."

"But by whom? By whom?"

"By his doctor."

"Who is this doctor?"

"I don't know. But one of M. Lavernoux's friends, an Englishman called Hargrove, the friend, in fact, with whom he was communicating, is bound to know and is also bound to know the exact and complete meaning of the communication, because, without waiting for the end, he jumped into a motor-cab and drove to the Prefecture of Police."

"Why? Why?... And what is the result of that step?"

"The result, monsieur le baron, is that your house is surrounded. There are twelve detectives under your windows. The moment the sun rises, they will enter in the name of the law and arrest the criminal."

"Then is Lavernoux's murderer concealed in my house? Who is he? One of the servants? But no, for you were speaking of a doctor!..."

"I would remark, monsieur le baron, that when this Mr. Hargrove went to the police to tell them of the revelations made by his friend Lavernoux, he was not aware that his friend Lavernoux was going to be murdered. The step taken by Mr. Hargrove had to do with something else...."

"With what?"

"With the disappearance of madame la baronne, of which he knew the secret, thanks to the communication made by Lavernoux."

"What! They know at last! They have found the baroness! Where is she? And the jewels? And the money she robbed me of?"

Baron Repstein was talking in a great state of excitement. He rose and, almost shouting at Lupin, cried:

"Finish your story, sir! I can't endure this suspense!"

Lupin continued, in a slow and hesitating voice:

"The fact is... you see... it is rather difficult to explain... for you and I are looking at the thing from a totally different point of view."

"I don't understand."

"And yet you ought to understand, monsieur le baron.... We begin by saying—I am quoting the newspapers—by saying, do we not, that Baroness Repstein knew all the secrets of your business and that she was able to open not only that safe over there, but also the one at the Crédit Lyonnais in which you kept your securities locked up?"

"Yes."

"Well, one evening, a fortnight ago, while you were at your club, Baroness Repstein, who, unknown to yourself, had converted all those securities into cash, left this house with a travelling-bag, containing your money and all the Princesse de Berny's jewels?"

"Yes."

"And, since then, she has not been seen?"

"No."

"Well, there is an excellent reason why she has not been seen."

"What reason?"

"This, that Baroness Repstein has been murdered...."

"Murdered!... The baroness!... But you're mad!"

"Murdered... and probably that same evening."

"I tell you again, you are mad! How can the baroness have been murdered, when the police are following her tracks, so to speak, step by step?"

"They are following the tracks of another woman."

"What woman?"

"The murderer's accomplice."

"And who is the murderer?"

"The same man who, for the last fortnight, knowing that Lavernoux, through the situation which he occupied in this house, had discovered the truth, kept him imprisoned, forced him to silence, threatened him, terrorized him; the same man who, finding Lavernoux in the act of communicating with a friend, made away with him in cold blood by stabbing him to the heart."

"The doctor, therefore?"

"Yes."

"But who is this doctor? Who is this malevolent genius, this infernal being who appears and disappears, who slays in the dark and whom nobody suspects?"

"Can't you guess?"

"No."

"And do you want to know?"

"Do I want to know?... Why, speak, man, speak!... You know where he is hiding?"

"Yes."

"In this house?"

"Yes."

"And it is he whom the police are after?"

"Yes."

"And I know him?"

"Yes."

"Who is it?"

"You!"

"I!..."

9

Lupin had not been more than ten minutes with the baron; and the duel was commencing. The accusation was hurled, definitely, violently, implacably.

Lupin repeated:

"You yourself, got up in a false beard and a pair of spectacles, bent in two, like an old man. In short, you, Baron Repstein; and it is you for a very good reason, of which nobody has thought, which is that, if it was not you who contrived the whole plot, the case becomes inexplicable. Whereas, taking you as the criminal, you as murdering the baroness in order to get rid of her and run through those millions with another woman, you as murdering Lavernoux, your agent, in order to suppress an unimpeachable witness, oh, then the whole case is explained! Well, is it pretty clear? And are not you yourself convinced?"

The baron, who, throughout this conversation, had stood bending over his visitor, waiting for each of his words with feverish avidity, now drew himself up and looked at Lupin as though he undoubtedly had to do with a madman. When Lupin had finished speaking, the baron stepped back two or three paces, seemed on the point of uttering words which he ended by not saying, and then, without taking his eyes from his strange visitor, went to the fireplace and rang the bell.

Lupin did not make a movement. He waited smiling.

The butler entered. His master said:

"You can go to bed, Antoine. I will let this gentleman out."

"Shall I put out the lights, sir?"

"Leave a light in the hall."

Antoine left the room and the baron, after taking a revolver from his desk, at once came back to Lupin, put the weapon in his pocket and said, very calmly:

"You must excuse this little precaution, sir. I am obliged to take it in case you should be mad, though that does not seem likely. No, you are not mad. But you have come here with an object which I fail to grasp; and you have sprung upon me an accusation of so astounding a character that I am curious to know the reason. I have experienced so much disappointment and undergone so much suffering that an outrage of this kind leaves me indifferent. Continue, please."

His voice shook with emotion and his sad eyes seemed moist with tears.

Lupin shuddered. Had he made a mistake? Was the surmise which his intuition had suggested to him and which was based upon a frail groundwork of slight facts, was this surmise wrong?

His attention was caught by a detail: through the opening in the baron's waistcoat he saw the point of the pin fixed in the tie and was thus able to realize the unusual length of the pin. Moreover, the gold stem was triangular and formed a sort of miniature dagger, very thin and very delicate, yet formidable in an expert hand.

And Lupin had no doubt but that the pin attached to that magnificent pearl was the weapon which had pierced the heart of the unfortunate M. Lavernoux.

He muttered:

"You're jolly clever, monsieur le baron!"

The other, maintaining a rather scornful gravity, kept silence, as though he did not understand and as though waiting for the explanation to which he felt himself entitled. And, in spite of everything, this impassive attitude worried Arsène Lupin. Nevertheless, his conviction was so profound and, besides, he had staked so much on the adventure that he repeated:

"Yes, jolly clever, for it is evident that the baroness only obeyed your orders in realizing your securities and also in borrowing the princess's jewels on the pretence of buying them. And it is evident that the person who walked out of your house with a bag was not your wife, but an accomplice, that chorus-girl probably, and that it is your chorus-girl who is deliberately allowing herself to be chased across the continent by our worthy Ganimard. And I look upon the trick as marvellous. What does the woman risk, seeing that it is the baroness who is being looked for? And how could they look for any other woman than the baroness, seeing that you have promised a reward of two hundred thousand francs to the person who finds the baroness?... Oh, that two hundred thousand francs lodged with a solicitor: what a stroke of genius! It has dazzled the police! It has thrown dust in the eyes of the most clear-sighted! A gentleman who lodges two hundred thousand francs with a solicitor is a gentleman who speaks the truth.... So they go on hunting the baroness! And they leave you quietly to settle your affairs, to sell your stud and your two houses to the highest bidder and to prepare your flight! Heavens, what a joke!"

The baron did not wince. He walked up to Lupin and asked, without abandoning his imperturbable coolness:

"Who are you?"

Lupin burst out laughing.

"What can it matter who I am? Take it that I am an emissary of fate, looming out of the darkness for your destruction!"

He sprang from his chair, seized the baron by the shoulder and jerked out:

"Yes, for your destruction, my bold baron! Listen to me! Your wife's three millions, almost all the princess's jewels, the money you received today from the sale of your stud and your real estate: it's all there, in your pocket, or in that safe. Your flight is prepared. Look, I can see the leather of your portmanteau behind that hanging. The papers on your desk are in order. This very night, you would have done a guy. This very night, disguised beyond recognition, after taking all your precautions, you would have joined your chorus-girl, the creature for whose sake you have committed murder, that same Nelly Darbal, no doubt, whom Ganimard arrested in Belgium. But for one sudden, unforeseen obstacle: the police, the twelve detectives who, thanks to Lavernoux's revelations, have been posted under your windows. They've cooked your goose, old chap!... Well, I'll save you. A word through the telephone; and, by three or four o'clock in the morning, twenty of my friends will have removed the obstacle, polished off the twelve detectives, and you and I will slip away quietly. My conditions? Almost nothing; a trifle to you: we share the millions and the jewels. Is it a bargain?"

He was leaning over the baron, thundering at him with irresistible energy. The baron whispered:

"I'm beginning to understand. It's blackmail...."

"Blackmail or not, call it what you please, my boy, but you've got to go through with it and do as I say. And don't imagine that I shall give way at the last moment. Don't say to yourself, 'Here's a gentleman whom the fear of the police will cause to think twice. If I run a big risk in refusing, he also will be risking the handcuffs, the cells and the rest of it, seeing that we are both being hunted down like wild beasts.' That would be a mistake, monsieur le baron. I can always get out of it. It's a question of yourself, of yourself alone.... Your money or your life, my lord! Share and share alike... if not, the scaffold! Is it a bargain?"

A quick movement. The baron released himself, grasped his revolver and fired.

But Lupin was prepared for the attack, the more so as the baron's face had lost its assurance and gradually, under the slow impulse of rage and fear, acquired an expression of almost bestial ferocity that heralded the rebellion so long kept under control.

He fired twice. Lupin first flung himself to one side and then dived at the baron's knees, seized him by both legs and brought him to the ground. The baron freed himself with an effort. The two enemies rolled over in each other's grip; and a stubborn, crafty, brutal, savage struggle followed.

Suddenly, Lupin felt a pain at his chest:

"You villain!" he yelled. "That's your Lavernoux trick; the tiepin!"

Stiffening his muscles with a desperate effort, he overpowered the baron and clutched him by the throat victorious at last and omnipotent.

"You ass!" he cried. "If you hadn't shown your cards, I might have thrown up the game! You have such a look of the honest man about you! But what a biceps, my lord!... I thought for a moment.... But it's all over, now!... Come, my friend, hand us the pin and look cheerful.... No, that's what I call pulling a face.... I'm holding you too tight, perhaps? My lord's at his last gasp?... Come, be good!... That's it, just a wee bit of string round the wrists; do you allow me?... Why, you and I are agreeing like two brothers! It's touching!... At heart, you know, I'm rather fond of you.... And now, my bonnie lad, mind yourself! And a thousand apologies!..."

Half raising himself, with all his strength he caught the other a terrible blow in the pit of the stomach. The baron gave a gurgle and lay stunned and unconscious.

"That comes of having a deficient sense of logic, my friend," said Lupin. "I offered you half your money. Now I'll give you none at all... provided I know where to find any of it. For that's the main thing. Where has the beggar hidden his dust? In the safe? By George, it'll be a tough job! Luckily, I have all the night before me...."

He began to feel in the baron's pockets, came upon a bunch of keys, first made sure that the portmanteau behind the curtain held no papers or jewels, and then went to the safe.

But, at that moment, he stopped short: he heard a noise somewhere. The servants? Impossible. Their attics were on the top floor. He listened. The noise came from below. And, suddenly, he understood: the detectives, who had heard the two shots, were banging at the front door, as was their duty, without waiting for daybreak. Then an electric bell rang, which Lupin recognized as that in the hall:

"By Jupiter!" he said. "Pretty work! Here are these jokers coming... and just as we were about to gather the fruits of our laborious efforts! Tut, tut, Lupin, keep cool! What's expected of you? To open a safe, of which you don't know the secret, in thirty seconds. That's a mere trifle to lose your head about! Come, all you have to do is to discover the secret! How many letters are there in the word? Four?"

He went on thinking, while talking and listening to the noise outside. He double-locked the door of the outer room and then came back to the safe:

"Four ciphers.... Four letters... four letters.... Who can lend me a hand?... Who can give me just a tiny hint?... Who? Why, Lavernoux, of course! That good Lavernoux, seeing that he took the trouble to indulge in optical telegraphy at the risk of his life.... Lord, what a fool I am!... Why, of course, why, of course, that's it!... By Jove, this is too exciting!... Lupin, you must count ten and suppress that distracted beating of your heart. If not, it means bad work."

He counted ten and, now quite calm, knelt in front of the safe. He turned the four knobs with careful attention. Next, he examined the bunch of keys, selected one of them, then another, and attempted, in vain, to insert them in the lock:

"There's luck in odd numbers," he muttered, trying a third key. "Victory! This is the right one! Open Sesame, good old Sesame, open!"

The lock turned. The door moved on its hinges. Lupin pulled it to him, after taking out the bunch of keys:

"The millions are ours," he said. "Baron, I forgive you!"

And then he gave a single bound backward, hiccoughing with fright. His legs staggered beneath him. The keys jingled together in his fevered hand with a sinister sound. And, for twenty, for thirty seconds, despite the din that was being raised and the electric bells that kept ringing through the house, he stood there, wild-eyed, gazing at the most horrible, the most abominable sight: a woman's body, half-dressed, bent in two in the safe, crammed in, like an overlarge parcel... and fair hair hanging down... and blood... clots of blood... and livid flesh, blue in places, decomposing, flaccid.

"The baroness!" he gasped. "The baroness!... Oh, the monster!..."

He roused himself from his torpor, suddenly, to spit in the murderer's face and pound him with his heels:

"Take that, you wretch!... Take that, you villain!... And, with it, the scaffold, the bran-basket!..."

Meanwhile, shouts came from the upper floors in reply to the detectives' ringing. Lupin heard footsteps scurrying down the stairs. It was time to think of beating a retreat.

In reality, this did not trouble him greatly. During his conversation with the baron, the enemy's extraordinary coolness had given him the feeling that there must be a private outlet. Besides, how could the baron have begun the fight, if he were not sure of escaping the police?

Lupin went into the next room. It looked out on the garden. At the moment when the detectives were entering the house, he flung his legs over the balcony and let himself down by a rain-pipe. He walked round the building. On the opposite side was a wall lined with shrubs. He slipped in between the shrubs and the wall and at once found a little door which he easily opened with one of the keys on the bunch. All that remained for him to do was to walk across a yard and pass through the empty rooms of a lodge; and in a few moments he found himself in the Rue du Faubourg Saint-Honoré. Of course—and this he had reckoned on—the police had not provided for this secret outlet.

"Well, what do you think of Baron Repstein?" cried Lupin, after giving me all the details of that tragic night. "What a dirty scoundrel! And how it teaches one to distrust appearances! I swear to you, the fellow looked a thoroughly honest man!"

"But what about the millions?" I asked. "The princess's jewels?"

"They were in the safe. I remember seeing the parcel."

"Well?"

"They are there still."

"Impossible!"

"They are, upon my word! I might tell you that I was afraid of the detectives, or else plead a sudden attack of delicacy. But the truth is simpler... and more prosaic: the smell was too awful!..."

"What?"

"Yes, my dear fellow, the smell that came from that safe... from that coffin.... No, I couldn't do it... my head swam.... Another second and I should have been ill.... Isn't it silly?... Look, this is all I got from my expedition: the tiepin.... The bedrock value of the pearl is thirty thousand francs.... But all the same, I feel jolly well annoyed. What a sell!"

"One more question," I said. "The word that opened the safe!"

"Well?"

"How did you guess it?"

"Oh, quite easily! In fact, I am surprised that I didn't think of it sooner."

"Well, tell me."

"It was contained in the revelations telegraphed by that poor Lavernoux."

"What?"

"Just think, my dear chap, the mistakes in spelling...."

"The mistakes in spelling?"

"Why, of course! They were deliberate. Surely, you don't imagine that the agent, the private secretary of the baron—who was a company-promoter, mind you, and a racing-man—did not know English better than to spell 'necessery' with an e, 'atack' with one t, 'ennemy' with two ns and 'prudance' with an a! The thing struck me at once. I put the four letters together and got 'Etna,' the name of the famous horse."

"And was that one word enough?"

"Of course! It was enough to start with, to put me on the scent of the Repstein case, of which all the papers were full, and, next, to make me guess that it was the key-word of the safe, because, on the one hand, Lavernoux knew the gruesome contents of the safe and, on the other, he was denouncing the baron. And it was in the same way that I was led to suppose that Lavernoux had a friend in the street, that they both frequented the same café, that they amused themselves by working out the problems and cryptograms in the illustrated papers and that they had contrived a way of exchanging telegrams from window to window."

"That makes it all quite simple!" I exclaimed.

"Very simple. And the incident once more shows that, in the discovery of crimes, there is something much more valuable than the examination of facts, than observations, deductions, inferences and all that stuff and nonsense. What I mean is, as I said before, intuition... intuition and intelligence.... And Arsène Lupin, without boasting, is deficient in neither one nor the other!..."

14

II

THE WEDDING-RING

Yvonne d'Origny kissed her son and told him to be good:

"You know your grandmother d'Origny is not very fond of children. Now that she has sent for you to come and see her, you must show her what a sensible little boy you are." And, turning to the governess, "Don't forget, Fräulein, to bring him home immediately after dinner.... Is monsieur still in the house?"

"Yes, madame, *monsieur le comte* is in his study."

As soon as she was alone, Yvonne d'Origny walked to the window to catch a glimpse of her son as he left the house. He was out in the street in a moment, raised his head and blew her a kiss, as was his custom every day. Then the governess took his hand with, as Yvonne remarked to her surprise, a movement of unusual violence. Yvonne leant further out of the window and, when the boy reached the corner of the boulevard, she suddenly saw a man step out of a motorcar and go up to him. The man, in whom she recognized Bernard, her husband's confidential servant, took the child by the arm, made both him and the governess get into the car, and ordered the chauffeur to drive off.

The whole incident did not take ten seconds.

Yvonne, in her trepidation, ran to her bedroom, seized a wrap and went to the door. The door was locked; and there was no key in the lock.

She hurried back to the boudoir. The door of the boudoir also was locked.

Then, suddenly, the image of her husband appeared before her, that gloomy face which no smile ever lit up, those pitiless eyes in which, for years, she had felt so much hatred and malice.

"It's he... it's he!" she said to herself. "He has taken the child.... Oh, it's horrible!"

She beat against the door with her fists, with her feet, then flew to the mantelpiece and pressed the bell fiercely.

The shrill sound rang through the house from top to bottom. The servants would be sure to come. Perhaps a crowd would gather in the street. And, impelled by a sort of despairing hope, she kept her finger on the button.

A key turned in the lock.... The door was flung wide open. The count appeared on the threshold of the boudoir. And the expression of his face was so terrible that Yvonne began to tremble.

He entered the room. Five or six steps separated him from her. With a supreme effort, she tried to stir, but all movement was impossible; and, when she attempted to speak, she could only flutter her lips and emit incoherent sounds. She felt herself lost. The thought of death unhinged her. Her knees gave way beneath her and she sank into a huddled heap, with a moan.

The count rushed at her and seized her by the throat:

"Hold your tongue... don't call out!" he said, in a low voice. "That will be best for you!..."

Seeing that she was not attempting to defend herself, he loosened his hold of her and took from his pocket some strips of canvas ready rolled and of different lengths. In a few minutes, Yvonne was lying on a sofa, with her wrists and ankles bound and her arms fastened close to her body.

It was now dark in the boudoir. The count switched on the electric light and went to a little writing-desk where Yvonne was accustomed to keep her letters. Not succeeding in opening it, he picked the lock with a bent wire, emptied the drawers and collected all the contents into a bundle, which he carried off in a cardboard file:

"Waste of time, eh?" he grinned. "Nothing but bills and letters of no importance.... No proof against you.... Tah! I'll keep my son for all that; and I swear before Heaven that I will not let him go!"

As he was leaving the room, he was joined, near the door, by his man Bernard. The two stopped and talked, in a low voice; but Yvonne heard these words spoken by the servant:

"I have had an answer from the working jeweller. He says he holds himself at my disposal."

And the count replied:

"The thing is put off until twelve o'clock midday, tomorrow. My mother has just telephoned to say that she could not come before."

Then Yvonne heard the key turn in the lock and the sound of steps going down to the ground-floor, where her husband's study was.

She long lay inert, her brain reeling with vague, swift ideas that burnt her in passing, like flames. She remembered her husband's infamous behaviour, his humiliating conduct to her, his threats, his plans for a divorce; and she gradually came to understand that she was the victim of a regular conspiracy, that the servants had been sent away until the following evening by their master's orders, that the governess had carried off her son by the count's instructions and with Bernard's assistance, that her son would not come back and that she would never see him again.

"My son!" she cried. "My son!..."

Exasperated by her grief, she stiffened herself, with every nerve, with every muscle tense, to make a violent effort. And she was astonished to find that her right hand, which the count had fastened too hurriedly, still retained a certain freedom.

Then a mad hope invaded her; and, slowly, patiently, she began the work of self-deliverance.

It was long in the doing. She needed a deal of time to widen the knot sufficiently and a deal of time afterward, when the hand was released, to undo those other bonds which tied her arms to her body and those which fastened her ankles.

Still, the thought of her son sustained her; and the last shackle fell as the clock struck eight. She was free!

She was no sooner on her feet than she flew to the window and flung back the latch, with the intention of calling the first passerby. At that moment a policeman came walking along the pavement. She leant out. But the brisk evening air, striking her face, calmed her. She thought of the scandal, of the judicial investigation, of the cross-examination, of her son. O Heaven! What could she do to get him back? How could she escape? The count might appear at the least sound. And who knew but that, in a moment of fury...?

She shivered from head to foot, seized with a sudden terror. The horror of death mingled, in her poor brain, with the thought of her son; and she stammered, with a choking throat:

"Help!... Help!..."

She stopped and said to herself, several times over, in a low voice, "Help!... Help!..." as though the word awakened an idea, a memory within her, and as though the hope of assistance no longer seemed to her impossible. For some minutes she remained absorbed in deep meditation, broken by fears and starts. Then, with an almost mechanical series of movements, she put out her arm to a little set of shelves hanging over the writing-desk, took down four books, one after the other, turned the pages with a distraught air, replaced them and ended by finding, between the pages of the fifth, a visiting-card on which her eyes spelt the name:

HORACE VELMONT,

followed by an address written in pencil:

CERCLE DE LA RUE ROYALE.

And her memory conjured up the strange thing which that man had said to her, a few years before, in that same house, on a day when she was at home to her friends:

"If ever a danger threatens you, if you need help, do not hesitate; post this card, which you see me put into this book; and, whatever the hour, whatever the obstacles, I will come."

With what a curious air he had spoken these words and how well he had conveyed the impression of certainty, of strength, of unlimited power, of indomitable daring!

Abruptly, unconsciously, acting under the impulse of an irresistible determination, the consequences of which she refused to anticipate, Yvonne, with the same automatic gestures, took a pneumatic-delivery envelope, slipped in the card, sealed it, directed it to "Horace Velmont, Cercle de la Rue Royale" and went to the open window. The policeman was walking up and down outside. She flung out the envelope, trusting to fate. Perhaps it would be picked up, treated as a lost letter and posted.

She had hardly completed this act when she realized its absurdity. It was mad to suppose that the message would reach the address and madder still to hope that the man to whom she was sending could come to her assistance, "whatever the hour, whatever the obstacles."

A reaction followed which was all the greater inasmuch as the effort had been swift and violent. Yvonne staggered, leant against a chair and, losing all energy, let herself fall.

The hours passed by, the dreary hours of winter evenings when nothing but the sound of carriages interrupts the silence of the street. The clock struck, pitilessly. In the half-sleep that numbed her limbs, Yvonne counted the strokes. She also heard certain noises, on different floors of the house, which told her that her husband had dined, that he was going up to his room, that he was going down again to his study. But all this seemed very shadowy to her; and her torpor was such that she did not even think of lying down on the sofa, in case he should come in....

The twelve strokes of midnight.... Then half-past twelve... then one.... Yvonne thought of nothing, awaiting the events which were preparing and against which rebellion was useless. She pictured her son and herself as one pictures those beings who have suffered much and who suffer no more and who take each other in their loving arms. But a nightmare shattered this dream. For now those two beings were to be torn asunder; and she had the awful feeling, in her delirium, that she was crying and choking....

She leapt from her seat. The key had turned in the lock. The count was coming, attracted by her cries. Yvonne glanced round for a weapon with which to defend herself. But the door was pushed back quickly and, astounded, as though the sight that presented itself before her eyes seemed to her the most inexplicable prodigy, she stammered:

"You!... You!..."

A man was walking up to her, in dress-clothes, with his opera-hat and cape under his arm, and this man, young, slender and elegant, she had recognized as Horace Velmont.

"You!" she repeated.

He said, with a bow:

"I beg your pardon, madame, but I did not receive your letter until very late."

"Is it possible? Is it possible that this is you... that you were able to...?"

He seemed greatly surprised:

"Did I not promise to come in answer to your call?"

"Yes... but..."

"Well, here I am," he said, with a smile.

He examined the strips of canvas from which Yvonne had succeeded in freeing herself and nodded his head, while continuing his inspection:

"So those are the means employed? The Comte d'Origny, I presume?... I also saw that he locked you in.... But then the pneumatic letter?... Ah, through the window!... How careless of you not to close it!"

He pushed both sides to. Yvonne took fright:

"Suppose they hear!"

"There is no one in the house. I have been over it."

"Still..."

"Your husband went out ten minutes ago."

"Where is he?"

"With his mother, the Comtesse d'Origny."

"How do you know?"

"Oh, it's very simple! He was rung up by telephone and I awaited the result at the corner of this street and the boulevard. As I expected, the count came out hurriedly, followed by his man. I at once entered, with the aid of special keys."

He told this in the most natural way, just as one tells a meaningless anecdote in a drawing-room. But Yvonne, suddenly seized with fresh alarm, asked:

"Then it's not true?... His mother is not ill?... In that case, my husband will be coming back...."

"Certainly, the count will see that a trick has been played on him and in three quarters of an hour at the latest...."

"Let us go.... I don't want him to find me here.... I must go to my son...."

"One moment...."

"One moment!... But don't you know that they have taken him from me?... That they are hurting him, perhaps?..."

With set face and feverish gestures, she tried to push Velmont back. He, with great gentleness, compelled her to sit down and, leaning over her in a respectful attitude, said, in a serious voice:

"Listen, madame, and let us not waste time, when every minute is valuable. First of all, remember this: we met four times, six years ago.... And, on the fourth occasion, when I was speaking to you, in the drawing-room of this house, with too much—what shall I say?—with too much feeling, you gave me to understand that my visits were no longer welcome. Since that day I have not seen you. And, nevertheless, in spite of all, your faith in me was such that you kept the card which I put between the pages of that book and, six years later, you send for me and none other. That faith in me I ask you to continue. You must obey me blindly. Just as I surmounted every obstacle to come to you, so I will save you, whatever the position may be."

Horace Velmont's calmness, his masterful voice, with the friendly intonation, gradually quieted the countess. Though still very weak, she gained a fresh sense of ease and security in that man's presence.

"Have no fear," he went on. "The Comtesse d'Origny lives at the other end of the Bois de Vincennes. Allowing that your husband finds a motor-cab, it is impossible for him to be back before a quarter-past three. Well, it is twenty-five to three now. I swear to take you away at three o'clock exactly and to take you to your son. But I will not go before I know everything."

"What am I to do?" she asked.

"Answer me and very plainly. We have twenty minutes. It is enough. But it is not too much."

"Ask me what you want to know."

"Do you think that the count had any... any murderous intentions?"

"No."

"Then it concerns your son?"

"Yes."

"He is taking him away, I suppose, because he wants to divorce you and marry another woman, a former friend of yours, whom you have turned out of your house. Is that it? Oh, I entreat you, answer me frankly! These are facts of public notoriety; and your hesitation, your scruples, must all cease, now that the matter concerns your son. So your husband wished to marry another woman?

"Yes."

"The woman has no money. Your husband, on his side, has gambled away all his property and has no means beyond the allowance which he receives from his mother, the Comtesse d'Origny, and the income of a large fortune which your son inherited from two of your uncles. It is this fortune which your husband covets and which he would appropriate more easily if the child were placed in his hands. There is only one way: divorce. Am I right?"

"Yes."

"And what has prevented him until now is your refusal?"

"Yes, mine and that of my mother-in-law, whose religious feelings are opposed to divorce. The Comtesse d'Origny would only yield in case..."

"In case...?"

19

"In case they could prove me guilty of shameful conduct."

Velmont shrugged his shoulders:

"Therefore he is powerless to do anything against you or against your son. Both from the legal point of view and from that of his own interests, he stumbles against an obstacle which is the most insurmountable of all: the virtue of an honest woman. And yet, in spite of everything, he suddenly shows fight."

"What do you mean?"

"I mean that, if a man like the count, after so many hesitations and in the face of so many difficulties, risks so doubtful an adventure, it must be because he thinks he has command of weapons..."

"What weapons?"

"I don't know. But they exist... or else he would not have begun by taking away your son."

Yvonne gave way to her despair:

"Oh, this is horrible!... How do I know what he may have done, what he may have invented?"

"Try and think.... Recall your memories.... Tell me, in this desk which he has broken open, was there any sort of letter which he could possibly turn against you?"

"No... only bills and addresses...."

"And, in the words he used to you, in his threats, is there nothing that allows you to guess?"

"Nothing."

"Still... still," Velmont insisted, "there must be something." And he continued, "Has the count a particularly intimate friend... in whom he confides?"

"No."

"Did anybody come to see him yesterday?"

"No, nobody."

"Was he alone when he bound you and locked you in?"

"At that moment, yes."

"But afterward?"

"His man, Bernard, joined him near the door and I heard them talking about a working jeweller...."

"Is that all?"

"And about something that was to happen the next day, that is, today, at twelve o'clock, because the Comtesse d'Origny could not come earlier."

Velmont reflected:

"Has that conversation any meaning that throws a light upon your husband's plans?"

"I don't see any."

"Where are your jewels?"

"My husband has sold them all."

"You have nothing at all left?"

"No."

"Not even a ring?"

"No," she said, showing her hands, "none except this."

"Which is your wedding-ring?"

"Which is my... wedding-...."

She stopped, nonplussed. Velmont saw her flush as she stammered:

"Could it be possible?... But no... no... he doesn't know...."

Velmont at once pressed her with questions and Yvonne stood silent, motionless, anxious-faced. At last, she replied, in a low voice:

"This is not my wedding-ring. One day, long ago, it dropped from the mantelpiece in my bedroom, where I had put it a minute before and, hunt for it as I might, I could not find it again. So I ordered another, without saying anything about it... and this is the one, on my hand...."

"Did the real ring bear the date of your wedding?"

"Yes... the 23rd of October."

"And the second?"

"This one has no date."

He perceived a slight hesitation in her and a confusion which, in point of fact, she did not try to conceal.

"I implore you," he exclaimed, "don't hide anything from me.... You see how far we have gone in a few minutes, with a little logic and calmness.... Let us go on, I ask you as a favour."

"Are you sure," she said, "that it is necessary?"

"I am sure that the least detail is of importance and that we are nearly attaining our object. But we must hurry. This is a crucial moment."

"I have nothing to conceal," she said, proudly raising her head. "It was the most wretched and the most dangerous period of my life. While suffering humiliation at home, outside I was surrounded with attentions, with temptations, with pitfalls, like any woman who is seen to be neglected by her husband. Then I remembered: before my marriage, a man had been in love with me. I had guessed his unspoken love; and he has died since. I had the name of that man engraved inside the ring; and I wore it as a talisman. There was no love in me, because I was the wife of another. But, in my secret heart, there was a memory, a sad dream, something sweet and gentle that protected me...."

She had spoken slowly, without embarrassment, and Velmont did not doubt for a second that she was telling the absolute truth. He kept silent; and she, becoming anxious again, asked:

"Do you suppose... that my husband...?"

He took her hand and, while examining the plain gold ring, said:

"The puzzle lies here. Your husband, I don't know how, knows of the substitution of one ring for the other. His mother will be here at twelve o'clock. In the presence of witnesses, he will compel you to take off your ring; and, in this way, he will obtain the approval of his mother and, at the same time, will be able to obtain his divorce, because he will have the proof for which he was seeking."

"I am lost!" she moaned. "I am lost!"

"On the contrary, you are saved! Give me that ring... and presently he will find another there, another which I will send you, to reach you before twelve, and which will bear the date of the 23rd of October. So...."

He suddenly broke off. While he was speaking, Yvonne's hand had turned ice-cold in his; and, raising his eyes, he saw that the young woman was pale, terribly pale:

21

"What's the matter? I beseech you…"

She yielded to a fit of mad despair:

"This is the matter, that I am lost!… This is the matter, that I can't get the ring off! It has grown too small for me!… Do you understand?… It made no difference and I did not give it a thought…. But today… this proof… this accusation…. Oh, what torture!… Look… it forms part of my finger… it has grown into my flesh… and I can't… I can't…."

She pulled at the ring, vainly, with all her might, at the risk of injuring herself. But the flesh swelled up around the ring; and the ring did not budge.

"Oh!" she cried, seized with an idea that terrified her. "I remember… the other night… a nightmare I had…. It seemed to me that someone entered my room and caught hold of my hand…. And I could not wake up…. It was he! It was he! He had put me to sleep, I was sure of it… and he was looking at the ring…. And presently he will pull it off before his mother's eyes…. Ah, I understand everything: that working jeweller!… He will cut it from my hand tomorrow…. You see, you see…. I am lost!…"

She hid her face in her hands and began to weep. But, amid the silence, the clock struck once… and twice… and yet once more. And Yvonne drew herself up with a jerk:

"There he is!" she cried. "He is coming!… It is three o'clock!… Let us go!…"

She grabbed at her cloak and ran to the door… Velmont barred the way and, in a masterful tone:

"You shall not go!"

"My son…. I want to see him, to take him back…."

"You don't even know where he is!"

"I want to go."

"You shall not go!… It would be madness…."

He took her by the wrists. She tried to release herself; and Velmont had to employ a little force to overcome her resistance. In the end, he succeeded in getting her back to the sofa, then in laying her at full length and, at once, without heeding her lamentations, he took the canvas strips and fastened her wrists and ankles:

"Yes," he said, "It would be madness! Who would have set you free? Who would have opened that door for you? An accomplice? What an argument against you and what a pretty use your husband would make of it with his mother!… And, besides, what's the good? To run away means accepting divorce… and what might that not lead to?… You must stay here…."

She sobbed:

"I'm frightened…. I'm frightened… this ring burns me…. Break it…. Take it away…. Don't let him find it!"

"And if it is not found on your finger, who will have broken it? Again an accomplice…. No, you must face the music… and face it boldly, for I answer for everything…. Believe me… I answer for everything…. If I have to tackle the Comtesse d'Origny bodily and thus delay the interview…. If I had to come myself before noon… it is the real wedding-ring that shall be taken from your finger—that I swear!—and your son shall be restored to you."

Swayed and subdued, Yvonne instinctively held out her hands to the bonds. When he stood up, she was bound as she had been before.

22

He looked round the room to make sure that no trace of his visit remained. Then he stooped over the countess again and whispered:

"Think of your son and, whatever happens, fear nothing.... I am watching over you."

She heard him open and shut the door of the boudoir and, a few minutes later, the hall-door.

At half-past three, a motor-cab drew up. The door downstairs was slammed again; and, almost immediately after, Yvonne saw her husband hurry in, with a furious look in his eyes. He ran up to her, felt to see if she was still fastened and, snatching her hand, examined the ring. Yvonne fainted....

She could not tell, when she woke, how long she had slept. But the broad light of day was filling the boudoir; and she perceived, at the first movement which she made, that her bonds were cut. Then she turned her head and saw her husband standing beside her, looking at her:

"My son... my son..." she moaned. "I want my son...."

He replied, in a voice of which she felt the jeering insolence:

"Our son is in a safe place. And, for the moment, it's a question not of him, but of you. We are face to face with each other, probably for the last time, and the explanation between us will be a very serious one. I must warn you that it will take place before my mother. Have you any objection?"

Yvonne tried to hide her agitation and answered:

"None at all."

"Can I send for her?"

"Yes. Leave me, in the meantime. I shall be ready when she comes."

"My mother is here."

"Your mother is here?" cried Yvonne, in dismay, remembering Horace Velmont's promise.

"What is there to astonish you in that?"

"And is it now... is it at once that you want to...?"

"Yes."

"Why?... Why not this evening?... Why not tomorrow?"

"Today and now," declared the count. "A rather curious incident happened in the course of last night, an incident which I cannot account for and which decided me to hasten the explanation. Don't you want something to eat first?"

"No... no...."

"Then I will go and fetch my mother."

He turned to Yvonne's bedroom. Yvonne glanced at the clock. It marked twenty-five minutes to eleven!

"Ah!" she said, with a shiver of fright.

Twenty-five minutes to eleven! Horace Velmont would not save her and nobody in the world and nothing in the world would save her, for there was no miracle that could place the wedding-ring upon her finger.

23

The count, returning with the Comtesse d'Origny, asked her to sit down. She was a tall, lank, angular woman, who had always displayed a hostile feeling to Yvonne. She did not even bid her daughter-in-law good morning, showing that her mind was made up as regards the accusation:

"I don't think," she said, "that we need speak at length. In two words, my son maintains...."

"I don't maintain, mother," said the count, "I declare. I declare on my oath that, three months ago, during the holidays, the upholsterer, when laying the carpet in this room and the boudoir, found the wedding-ring which I gave my wife lying in a crack in the floor. Here is the ring. The date of the 23rd of October is engraved inside."

"Then," said the countess, "the ring which your wife carries...."

"That is another ring, which she ordered in exchange for the real one. Acting on my instructions, Bernard, my man, after long searching, ended by discovering in the outskirts of Paris, where he now lives, the little jeweller to whom she went. This man remembers perfectly and is willing to bear witness that his customer did not tell him to engrave a date, but a name. He has forgotten the name, but the man who used to work with him in his shop may be able to remember it. This working jeweller has been informed by letter that I required his services and he replied yesterday, placing himself at my disposal. Bernard went to fetch him at nine o'clock this morning. They are both waiting in my study."

He turned to his wife:

"Will you give me that ring of your own free will?"

"You know," she said, "from the other night, that it won't come off my finger."

"In that case, can I have the man up? He has the necessary implements with him."

"Yes," she said, in a voice faint as a whisper.

She was resigned. She conjured up the future as in a vision: the scandal, the decree of divorce pronounced against herself, the custody of the child awarded to the father; and she accepted this, thinking that she would carry off her son, that she would go with him to the ends of the earth and that the two of them would live alone together and happy....

Her mother-in-law said:

"You have been very thoughtless, Yvonne."

Yvonne was on the point of confessing to her and asking for her protection. But what was the good? How could the Comtesse d'Origny possibly believe her innocent? She made no reply.

Besides, the count at once returned, followed by his servant and by a man carrying a bag of tools under his arm.

And the count said to the man:

"You know what you have to do?"

"Yes," said the workman. "It's to cut a ring that's grown too small.... That's easily done.... A touch of the nippers...."

"And then you will see," said the count, "if the inscription inside the ring was the one you engraved."

Yvonne looked at the clock. It was ten minutes to eleven. She seemed to hear, somewhere in the house, a sound of voices raised in argument; and, in spite of herself, she felt a thrill of hope. Perhaps Velmont has succeeded.... But the sound was renewed;

and she perceived that it was produced by some costermongers passing under her window and moving farther on.

It was all over. Horace Velmont had been unable to assist her. And she understood that, to recover her child, she must rely upon her own strength, for the promises of others are vain.

She made a movement of recoil. She had felt the workman's heavy hand on her hand; and that hateful touch revolted her.

The man apologized, awkwardly. The count said to his wife:

"You must make up your mind, you know."

Then she put out her slim and trembling hand to the workman, who took it, turned it over and rested it on the table, with the palm upward. Yvonne felt the cold steel. She longed to die, then and there; and, at once attracted by that idea of death, she thought of the poisons which she would buy and which would send her to sleep almost without her knowing it.

The operation did not take long. Inserted on the slant, the little steel pliers pushed back the flesh, made room for themselves and bit the ring. A strong effort... and the ring broke. The two ends had only to be separated to remove the ring from the finger. The workman did so.

The count exclaimed, in triumph:

"At last! Now we shall see!... The proof is there! And we are all witnesses...."

He snatched up the ring and looked at the inscription. A cry of amazement escaped him. The ring bore the date of his marriage to Yvonne: "23rd of October"!...

We were sitting on the terrace at Monte Carlo. Lupin finished his story, lit a cigarette and calmly puffed the smoke into the blue air.

I said:

"Well?"

"Well what?"

"Why, the end of the story...."

"The end of the story? But what other end could there be?"

"Come... you're joking..."

"Not at all. Isn't that enough for you? The countess is saved. The count, not possessing the least proof against her, is compelled by his mother to forego the divorce and to give up the child. That is all. Since then, he has left his wife, who is living happily with her son, a fine lad of sixteen."

"Yes... yes... but the way in which the countess was saved?"

Lupin burst out laughing:

"My dear old chap"—Lupin sometimes condescends to address me in this affectionate manner—"my dear old chap, you may be rather smart at relating my exploits, but, by Jove, you do want to have the *i*'s dotted for you! I assure you, the countess did not ask for explanations!"

"Very likely. But there's no pride about me," I added, laughing. "Dot those *i*'s for me, will you?"

He took out a five-franc piece and closed his hand over it.

"What's in my hand?"

"A five-franc piece."

He opened his hand. The five-franc piece was gone.

"You see how easy it is! A working jeweller, with his nippers, cuts a ring with a date engraved upon it: 23rd of October. It's a simple little trick of sleight-of-hand, one of many which I have in my bag. By Jove, I didn't spend six months with Dickson, the conjurer, for nothing!"

"But then...?"

"Out with it!"

"The working jeweller?"

"Was Horace Velmont! Was good old Lupin! Leaving the countess at three o'clock in the morning, I employed the few remaining minutes before the husband's return to have a look round his study. On the table I found the letter from the working jeweller. The letter gave me the address. A bribe of a few louis enabled me to take the workman's place; and I arrived with a wedding-ring ready cut and engraved. Hocus-pocus! Pass!... The count couldn't make head or tail of it."

"Splendid!" I cried. And I added, a little chaffingly, in my turn, "But don't you think that you were humbugged a bit yourself, on this occasion?"

"Oh! And by whom, pray?"

"By the countess?"

"In what way?"

"Hang it all, that name engraved as a talisman!... The mysterious Adonis who loved her and suffered for her sake!... All that story seems very unlikely; and I wonder whether, Lupin though you be, you did not just drop upon a pretty love-story, absolutely genuine and... none too innocent."

Lupin looked at me out of the corner of his eye:

"No," he said.

"How do you know?"

"If the countess made a misstatement in telling me that she knew that man before her marriage—and that he was dead—and if she really did love him in her secret heart, I, at least, have a positive proof that it was an ideal love and that he did not suspect it."

"And where is the proof?"

"It is inscribed inside the ring which I myself broke on the countess's finger... and which I carry on me. Here it is. You can read the name she had engraved on it."

He handed me the ring. I read:

"Horace Velmont."

There was a moment of silence between Lupin and myself; and, noticing it, I also observed on his face a certain emotion, a tinge of melancholy.

I resumed:

"What made you tell me this story... to which you have often alluded in my presence?"

"What made me...?"

He drew my attention to a woman, still exceedingly handsome, who was passing on a young man's arm. She saw Lupin and bowed.

"It's she," he whispered. "She and her son."

"Then she recognized you?"

"She always recognizes me, whatever my disguise."

"But since the burglary at the Château de Thibermesnil, the police have identified the two names of Arsène Lupin and Horace Velmont."

"Yes."

"Therefore she knows who you are."

"Yes."

"And she bows to you?" I exclaimed, in spite of myself.

He caught me by the arm and, fiercely:

"Do you think that I am Lupin to her? Do you think that I am a burglar in her eyes, a rogue, a cheat?... Why, I might be the lowest of miscreants, I might be a murderer even... and still she would bow to me!"

"Why? Because she loved you once?"

"Rot! That would be an additional reason, on the contrary, why she should now despise me."

"What then?"

"I am the man who gave her back her son!"

III

THE SIGN OF THE SHADOW

"I received your telegram and here I am," said a gentleman with a grey moustache, who entered my study, dressed in a dark-brown frock-coat and a wide-brimmed hat, with a red ribbon in his buttonhole. "What's the matter?"

Had I not been expecting Arsène Lupin, I should certainly never have recognized him in the person of this old half-pay officer:

"What's the matter?" I echoed. "Oh, nothing much: a rather curious coincidence, that's all. And, as I know that you would just as soon clear up a mystery as plan one...."

"Well?"

"You seem in a great hurry!"

"I am... unless the mystery in question is worth putting myself out for. So let us get to the point."

"Very well. Just begin by casting your eye on this little picture, which I picked up, a week or two ago, in a grimy old shop on the other side of the river. I bought it for the sake of its Empire frame, with the palm-leaf ornaments on the mouldings... for the painting is execrable."

"Execrable, as you say," said Lupin, after he had examined it, "but the subject itself is rather nice. That corner of an old courtyard, with its rotunda of Greek columns, its sundial and its fishpond and that ruined well with the Renaissance roof and those stone steps and stone benches: all very picturesque."

"And genuine," I added. "The picture, good or bad, has never been taken out of its Empire frame. Besides, it is dated.... There, in the left-hand bottom corner: those red figures, 15. 4. 2, which obviously stand for 15 April, 1802."

"I dare say... I dare say.... But you were speaking of a coincidence and, so far, I fail to see...."

I went to a corner of my study, took a telescope, fixed it on its stand and pointed it, through the open window, at the open window of a little room facing my flat, on the other side of the street. And I asked Lupin to look through it.

He stooped forward. The slanting rays of the morning sun lit up the room opposite, revealing a set of mahogany furniture, all very simple, a large bed and a child's bed hung with cretonne curtains.

"Ah!" cried Lupin, suddenly. "The same picture!"

"Exactly the same!" I said. "And the date: do you see the date, in red? 15. 4. 2."

"Yes, I see.... And who lives in that room?"

"A lady... or, rather, a workwoman, for she has to work for her living... needlework, hardly enough to keep herself and her child."

"What is her name?"

"Louise d'Ernemont…. From what I hear, she is the great-granddaughter of a farmer-general who was guillotined during the Terror."

"Yes, on the same day as André Chénier," said Lupin. "According to the memoirs of the time, this d'Ernemont was supposed to be a very rich man." He raised his head and said, "It's an interesting story…. Why did you wait before telling me?"

"Because this is the 15th of April."

"Well?"

"Well, I discovered yesterday—I heard them talking about it in the porter's box—that the 15th of April plays an important part in the life of Louise d'Ernemont."

"Nonsense!"

"Contrary to her usual habits, this woman who works every day of her life, who keeps her two rooms tidy, who cooks the lunch which her little girl eats when she comes home from the parish school… this woman, on the 15th of April, goes out with the child at ten o'clock in the morning and does not return until nightfall. And this has happened for years and in all weathers. You must admit that there is something queer about this date which I find on an old picture, which is inscribed on another, similar picture and which controls the annual movements of the descendant of d'Ernemont the farmer-general."

"Yes, it's curious… you're quite right," said Lupin, slowly. "And don't you know where she goes to?"

"Nobody knows. She does not confide in a soul. As a matter of fact, she talks very little."

"Are you sure of your information?"

"Absolutely. And the best proof of its accuracy is that here she comes."

A door had opened at the back of the room opposite, admitting a little girl of seven or eight, who came and looked out of the window. A lady appeared behind her, tall, good-looking still and wearing a sad and gentle air. Both of them were ready and dressed, in clothes which were simple in themselves, but which pointed to a love of neatness and a certain elegance on the part of the mother.

"You see," I whispered, "they are going out."

And presently the mother took the child by the hand and they left the room together.

Lupin caught up his hat:

"Are you coming?"

My curiosity was too great for me to raise the least objection. I went downstairs with Lupin.

As we stepped into the street, we saw my neighbour enter a baker's shop. She bought two rolls and placed them in a little basket which her daughter was carrying and which seemed already to contain some other provisions. Then they went in the direction of the outer boulevards and followed them as far as the Place de l'Étoile, where they turned down the Avenue Kléber to walk toward Passy.

Lupin strolled silently along, evidently obsessed by a train of thought which I was glad to have provoked. From time to time, he uttered a sentence which showed me the thread of his reflections; and I was able to see that the riddle remained as much a mystery to him as to myself.

Louise d'Ernemont, meanwhile, had branched off to the left, along the Rue Raynouard, a quiet old street in which Franklin and Balzac once lived, one of those streets which, lined with old-fashioned houses and walled gardens, give you the impression of being in a country-town. The Seine flows at the foot of the slope which the street crowns; and a number of lanes run down to the river.

My neighbour took one of these narrow, winding, deserted lanes. The first building, on the right, was a house the front of which faced the Rue Raynouard. Next came a moss-grown wall, of a height above the ordinary, supported by buttresses and bristling with broken glass.

Halfway along the wall was a low, arched door. Louise d'Ernemont stopped in front of this door and opened it with a key which seemed to us enormous. Mother and child entered and closed the door.

"In any case," said Lupin, "she has nothing to conceal, for she has not looked round once...."

He had hardly finished his sentence when we heard the sound of footsteps behind us. It was two old beggars, a man and a woman, tattered, dirty, squalid, covered in rags. They passed us without paying the least attention to our presence. The man took from his wallet a key similar to my neighbour's and put it into the lock. The door closed behind them.

And, suddenly, at the top of the lane, came the noise of a motorcar stopping.... Lupin dragged me fifty yards lower down, to a corner in which we were able to hide. And we saw coming down the lane, carrying a little dog under her arm, a young and very much overdressed woman, wearing a quantity of jewellery, a young woman whose eyes were too dark, her lips too red, her hair too fair. In front of the door, the same performance, with the same key.... The lady and the dog disappeared from view.

"This promises to be most amusing," said Lupin, chuckling. "What earthly connection can there be between those different people?"

There hove in sight successively two elderly ladies, lean and rather poverty-stricken in appearance, very much alike, evidently sisters; a footman in livery; an infantry corporal; a fat gentleman in a soiled and patched jacket-suit; and, lastly, a workman's family, father, mother, and four children, all six of them pale and sickly, looking like people who never eat their fill. And each of the newcomers carried a basket or string-bag filled with provisions.

"It's a picnic!" I cried.

"It grows more and more surprising," said Lupin, "and I shan't be satisfied till I know what is happening behind that wall."

To climb it was out of the question. We also saw that it finished, at the lower as well as at the upper end, at a house none of whose windows overlooked the enclosure which the wall contained.

During the next hour, no one else came along. We vainly cast about for a stratagem; and Lupin, whose fertile brain had exhausted every possible expedient, was about to go in search of a ladder, when, suddenly, the little door opened and one of the workman's children came out.

The boy ran up the lane to the Rue Raynouard. A few minutes later he returned, carrying two bottles of water, which he set down on the pavement to take the big key from his pocket.

By that time Lupin had left me and was strolling slowly along the wall. When the child, after entering the enclosure, pushed back the door Lupin sprang forward and stuck the point of his knife into the staple of the lock. The bolt failed to catch; and it became an easy matter to push the door ajar.

"That's done the trick!" said Lupin.

He cautiously put his hand through the doorway and then, to my great surprise, entered boldly. But, on following his example, I saw that, ten yards behind the wall, a clump of laurels formed a sort of curtain which allowed us to come up unobserved.

Lupin took his stand right in the middle of the clump. I joined him and, like him, pushed aside the branches of one of the shrubs. And the sight which presented itself to my eyes was so unexpected that I was unable to suppress an exclamation, while Lupin, on his side, muttered, between his teeth:

"By Jupiter! This is a funny job!"

We saw before us, within the confined space that lay between the two windowless houses, the identical scene represented in the old picture which I had bought at a secondhand dealer's!

The identical scene! At the back, against the opposite wall, the same Greek rotunda displayed its slender columns. In the middle, the same stone benches topped a circle of four steps that ran down to a fishpond with moss-grown flags. On the left, the same well raised its wrought-iron roof; and, close at hand, the same sundial showed its slanting gnomon and its marble face.

The identical scene! And what added to the strangeness of the sight was the memory, obsessing Lupin and myself, of that date of the 15th of April, inscribed in a corner of the picture, and the thought that this very day was the 15th of April and that sixteen or seventeen people, so different in age, condition and manners, had chosen the 15th of April to come together in this forgotten corner of Paris!

All of them, at the moment when we caught sight of them, were sitting in separate groups on the benches and steps; and all were eating. Not very far from my neighbour and her daughter, the workman's family and the beggar couple were sharing their provisions; while the footman, the gentleman in the soiled suit, the infantry corporal and the two lean sisters were making a common stock of their sliced ham, their tins of sardines and their gruyère cheese.

The lady with the little dog alone, who had brought no food with her, sat apart from the others, who made a show of turning their backs upon her. But Louise d'Ernemont offered her a sandwich, whereupon her example was followed by the two sisters; and the corporal at once began to make himself as agreeable to the young person as he could.

It was now half-past one. The beggar-man took out his pipe, as did the fat gentleman; and, when they found that one had no tobacco and the other no matches, their needs soon brought them together. The men went and smoked by the rotunda and the women joined them. For that matter, all these people seemed to know one another quite well.

They were at some distance from where we were standing, so that we could not hear what they said. However, we gradually perceived that the conversation was becoming animated. The young person with the dog, in particular, who by this time appeared to be in great request, indulged in much voluble talk, accompanying her words with many gestures, which set the little dog barking furiously.

But, suddenly, there was an outcry, promptly followed by shouts of rage; and one and all, men and women alike, rushed in disorder toward the well. One of the workman's brats was at that moment coming out of it, fastened by his belt to the hook at the end of the rope; and the three other urchins were drawing him up by turning the handle. More active than the rest, the corporal flung himself upon him; and forthwith the footman and the fat gentleman seized hold of him also, while the beggars and the lean sisters came to blows with the workman and his family.

In a few seconds the little boy had not a stitch left on him beyond his shirt. The footman, who had taken possession of the rest of the clothes, ran away, pursued by the corporal, who snatched away the boy's breeches, which were next torn from the corporal by one of the lean sisters.

"They are mad!" I muttered, feeling absolutely at sea.

"Not at all, not at all," said Lupin.

"What! Do you mean to say that you can make head or tail of what is going on?"

He did not reply. The young lady with the little dog, tucking her pet under her arm, had started running after the child in the shirt, who uttered loud yells. The two of them raced round the laurel-clump in which we stood hidden; and the brat flung himself into his mother's arms.

At long last, Louise d'Ernemont, who had played a conciliatory part from the beginning, succeeded in allaying the tumult. Everybody sat down again; but there was a reaction in all those exasperated people and they remained motionless and silent, as though worn out with their exertions.

And time went by. Losing patience and beginning to feel the pangs of hunger, I went to the Rue Raynouard to fetch something to eat, which we divided while watching the actors in the incomprehensible comedy that was being performed before our eyes. They hardly stirred. Each minute that passed seemed to load them with increasing melancholy; and they sank into attitudes of discouragement, bent their backs more and more and sat absorbed in their meditations.

The afternoon wore on in this way, under a grey sky that shed a dreary light over the enclosure.

"Are they going to spend the night here?" I asked, in a bored voice.

But, at five o'clock or so, the fat gentleman in the soiled jacket-suit took out his watch. The others did the same and all, watch in hand, seemed to be anxiously awaiting an event of no little importance to themselves. The event did not take place, for, in fifteen or twenty minutes, the fat gentleman gave a gesture of despair, stood up and put on his hat.

Then lamentations broke forth. The two lean sisters and the workman's wife fell upon their knees and made the sign of the cross. The lady with the little dog and the beggar-woman kissed each other and sobbed; and we saw Louise d'Ernemont pressing her daughter sadly to her.

"Let's go," said Lupin.

"You think it's over?"

"Yes; and we have only just time to make ourselves scarce."

We went out unmolested. At the top of the lane, Lupin turned to the left and, leaving me outside, entered the first house in the Rue Raynouard, the one that backed on to the enclosure.

After talking for a few seconds to the porter, he joined me and we stopped a passing taxicab:

"No. 34 Rue de Turin," he said to the driver.

The ground-floor of No. 34 was occupied by a notary's office; and we were shown in, almost without waiting, to Maître Valandier, a smiling, pleasant-spoken man of a certain age.

Lupin introduced himself by the name of Captain Jeanniot, retired from the army. He said that he wanted to build a house to his own liking and that someone had suggested to him a plot of ground situated near the Rue Raynouard.

"But that plot is not for sale," said Maître Valandier.

"Oh, I was told...."

"You have been misinformed, I fear."

The lawyer rose, went to a cupboard and returned with a picture which he showed us. I was petrified. It was the same picture which I had bought, the same picture that hung in Louise d'Ernemont's room.

"This is a painting," he said, "of the plot of ground to which you refer. It is known as the Clos d'Ernemont."

"Precisely."

"Well, this close," continued the notary, "once formed part of a large garden belonging to d'Ernemont, the farmer-general, who was executed during the Terror. All that could be sold has been sold, piecemeal, by the heirs. But this last plot has remained and will remain in their joint possession... unless...."

The notary began to laugh.

"Unless what?" asked Lupin.

"Well, it's quite a romance, a rather curious romance, in fact. I often amuse myself by looking through the voluminous documents of the case."

"Would it be indiscreet, if I asked...?"

"Not at all, not at all," declared Maître Valandier, who seemed delighted, on the contrary, to have found a listener for his story. And, without waiting to be pressed, he began: "At the outbreak of the Revolution, Louis Agrippa d'Ernemont, on the pretence of joining his wife, who was staying at Geneva with their daughter Pauline, shut up his mansion in the Faubourg Saint-Germain, dismissed his servants and, with his son Charles, came and took up his abode in his pleasure-house at Passy, where he was known to nobody except an old and devoted serving-woman. He remained there in hiding for three years and he had every reason to hope that his retreat would not be discovered, when, one day, after luncheon, as he was having a nap, the old servant burst into his room. She had seen, at the end of the street, a patrol of armed men who seemed to be making for the house. Louis d'Ernemont got ready quickly and, at the moment when the men were knocking at the front door, disappeared through the door that led to the garden, shouting to his son, in a scared voice, to keep them talking, if only for five minutes. He may have intended to escape and found the outlets through the garden watched. In any case, he returned in six or seven minutes, replied very calmly to the questions put to him and raised no difficulty about accompanying the men. His son Charles, although only eighteen years of age, was arrested also."

"When did this happen?" asked Lupin.

"It happened on the 26th day of Germinal, Year II, that is to say, on the...."

Maître Valandier stopped, with his eyes fixed on a calendar that hung on the wall, and exclaimed:

"Why, it was on this very day! This is the 15th of April, the anniversary of the farmer-general's arrest."

"What an odd coincidence!" said Lupin. "And considering the period at which it took place, the arrest, no doubt, had serious consequences?"

"Oh, most serious!" said the notary, laughing. "Three months later, at the beginning of Thermidor, the farmer-general mounted the scaffold. His son Charles was forgotten in prison and their property was confiscated."

"The property was immense, I suppose?" said Lupin.

"Well, there you are! That's just where the thing becomes complicated. The property, which was, in fact, immense, could never be traced. It was discovered that the Faubourg Saint-Germain mansion had been sold, before the Revolution, to an Englishman, together with all the country-seats and estates and all the jewels, securities and collections belonging to the farmer-general. The Convention instituted minute inquiries, as did the Directory afterward. But the inquiries led to no result."

"There remained, at any rate, the Passy house," said Lupin.

"The house at Passy was bought, for a mere song, by a delegate of the Commune, the very man who had arrested d'Ernemont, one Citizen Broquet. Citizen Broquet shut himself up in the house, barricaded the doors, fortified the walls and, when Charles d'Ernemont was at last set free and appeared outside, received him by firing a musket at him. Charles instituted one lawsuit after another, lost them all and then proceeded to offer large sums of money. But Citizen Broquet proved intractable. He had bought the house and he stuck to the house; and he would have stuck to it until his death, if Charles had not obtained the support of Bonaparte. Citizen Broquet cleared out on the 12th of February, 1803; but Charles d'Ernemont's joy was so great and his brain, no doubt, had been so violently unhinged by all that he had gone through, that, on reaching the threshold of the house of which he had at last recovered the ownership, even before opening the door he began to dance and sing in the street. He had gone clean off his head."

"By Jove!" said Lupin. "And what became of him?"

"His mother and his sister Pauline, who had ended by marrying a cousin of the same name at Geneva, were both dead. The old servant-woman took care of him and they lived together in the Passy house. Years passed without any notable event; but, suddenly, in 1812, an unexpected incident happened. The old servant made a series of strange revelations on her deathbed, in the presence of two witnesses whom she sent for. She declared that the farmer-general had carried to his house at Passy a number of bags filled with gold and silver and that those bags had disappeared a few days before the arrest. According to earlier confidences made by Charles d'Ernemont, who had them from his father, the treasures were hidden in the garden, between the rotunda, the sundial and the well. In proof of her statement, she produced three pictures, or rather, for they were not yet framed, three canvases, which the farmer-general had painted during his captivity and which he had succeeded in conveying to her, with instructions to hand them to his wife, his son and his daughter. Tempted by the lure of wealth, Charles and the old servant had kept silence. Then came the lawsuits, the recovery of the house, Charles's madness, the servant's own useless searches; and the treasures were still there."

"And they are there now," chuckled Lupin.

"And they will be there always," exclaimed Maître Valandier. "Unless... unless Citizen Broquet, who no doubt smelt a rat, succeeded in ferreting them out. But this is an unlikely supposition, for Citizen Broquet died in extreme poverty."

"So then...?"

"So then everybody began to hunt. The children of Pauline, the sister, hastened from Geneva. It was discovered that Charles had been secretly married and that he had sons. All these heirs set to work."

"But Charles himself?"

"Charles lived in the most absolute retirement. He did not leave his room."

"Never?"

"Well, that is the most extraordinary, the most astounding part of the story. Once a year, Charles d'Ernemont, impelled by a sort of subconscious willpower, came downstairs, took the exact road which his father had taken, walked across the garden and sat down either on the steps of the rotunda, which you see here, in the picture, or on the kerb of the well. At twenty-seven minutes past five, he rose and went indoors again; and until his death, which occurred in 1820, he never once failed to perform this incomprehensible pilgrimage. Well, the day on which this happened was invariably the 15th of April, the anniversary of the arrest."

Maître Valandier was no longer smiling and himself seemed impressed by the amazing story which he was telling us.

"And, since Charles's death?" asked Lupin, after a moment's reflection.

"Since that time," replied the lawyer, with a certain solemnity of manner, "for nearly a hundred years, the heirs of Charles and Pauline d'Ernemont have kept up the pilgrimage of the 15th of April. During the first few years they made the most thorough excavations. Every inch of the garden was searched, every clod of ground dug up. All this is now over. They take hardly any pains. All they do is, from time to time, for no particular reason, to turn over a stone or explore the well. For the most part, they are content to sit down on the steps of the rotunda, like the poor madman; and, like him, they wait. And that, you see, is the sad part of their destiny. In those hundred years, all these people who have succeeded one another, from father to son, have lost—what shall I say?—the energy of life. They have no courage left, no initiative. They wait. They wait for the 15th of April; and, when the 15th of April comes, they wait for a miracle to take place. Poverty has ended by overtaking every one of them. My predecessors and I have sold first the house, in order to build another which yields a better rent, followed by bits of the garden and further bits. But, as to that corner over there," pointing to the picture, "they would rather die than sell it. On this they are all agreed: Louise d'Ernemont, who is the direct heiress of Pauline, as well as the beggars, the workman, the footman, the circus-rider and so on, who represent the unfortunate Charles."

There was a fresh pause; and Lupin asked:

"What is your own opinion, Maître Valandier?"

"My private opinion is that there's nothing in it. What credit can we give to the statements of an old servant enfeebled by age? What importance can we attach to the crotchets of a madman? Besides, if the farmer-general had realized his fortune, don't you think that that fortune would have been found? One could manage to hide a paper, a document, in a confined space like that, but not treasures."

"Still, the pictures?..."

"Yes, of course. But, after all, are they a sufficient proof?"

Lupin bent over the copy which the solicitor had taken from the cupboard and, after examining it at length, said:

"You spoke of three pictures."

"Yes, the one which you see was handed to my predecessor by the heirs of Charles. Louise d'Ernemont possesses another. As for the third, no one knows what became of it."

Lupin looked at me and continued:

"And do they all bear the same date?"

"Yes, the date inscribed by Charles d'Ernemont when he had them framed, not long before his death.... The same date, that is to say the 15th of April, Year II, according to the revolutionary calendar, as the arrest took place in April, 1794."

"Oh, yes, of course," said Lupin. "The figure 2 means...."

He thought for a few moments and resumed:

"One more question, if I may. Did no one ever come forward to solve the problem?"

Maître Valandier threw up his arms:

"Goodness gracious me!" he cried. "Why, it was the plague of the office! One of my predecessors, Maître Turbon, was summoned to Passy no fewer than eighteen times, between 1820 and 1843, by the groups of heirs, whom fortune-tellers, clairvoyants, visionaries, impostors of all sorts had promised that they would discover the farmer-general's treasures. At last, we laid down a rule: any outsider applying to institute a search was to begin by depositing a certain sum."

"What sum?"

"A thousand francs."

"And did this have the effect of frightening them off?"

"No. Four years ago, an Hungarian hypnotist tried the experiment and made me waste a whole day. After that, we fixed the deposit at five thousand francs. In case of success, a third of the treasure goes to the finder. In case of failure, the deposit is forfeited to the heirs. Since then, I have been left in peace."

"Here are your five thousand francs."

The lawyer gave a start:

"Eh? What do you say?"

"I say," repeated Lupin, taking five banknotes from his pocket and calmly spreading them on the table, "I say that here is the deposit of five thousand francs. Please give me a receipt and invite all the d'Ernemont heirs to meet me at Passy on the 15th of April next year."

The notary could not believe his senses. I myself, although Lupin had accustomed me to these surprises, was utterly taken back.

"Are you serious?" asked Maître Valandier.

"Perfectly serious."

"But, you know, I told you my opinion. All these improbable stories rest upon no evidence of any kind."

"I don't agree with you," said Lupin.

The notary gave him the look which we give to a person who is not quite right in his head. Then, accepting the situation, he took his pen and drew up a contract on stamped paper, acknowledging the payment of the deposit by Captain Jeanniot and promising him a third of such moneys as he should discover:

"If you change your mind," he added, "you might let me know a week before the time comes. I shall not inform the d'Ernemont family until the last moment, so as not to give those poor people too long a spell of hope."

"You can inform them this very day, Maître Valandier. It will make them spend a happier year."

We said goodbye. Outside, in the street, I cried:

"So you have hit upon something?"

"I?" replied Lupin. "Not a bit of it! And that's just what amuses me."

"But they have been searching for a hundred years!"

"It is not so much a matter of searching as of thinking. Now I have three hundred and sixty-five days to think in. It is a great deal more than I want; and I am afraid that I shall forget all about the business, interesting though it may be. Oblige me by reminding me, will you?"

I reminded him of it several times during the following months, though he never seemed to attach much importance to the matter. Then came a long period during which I had no opportunity of seeing him. It was the period, as I afterward learnt, of his visit to Armenia and of the terrible struggle on which he embarked against Abdul the Damned, a struggle which ended in the tyrant's downfall.

I used to write to him, however, at the address which he gave me and I was thus able to send him certain particulars which I had succeeded in gathering, here and there, about my neighbour Louise d'Ernemont, such as the love which she had conceived, a few years earlier, for a very rich young man, who still loved her, but who had been compelled by his family to throw her over; the young widow's despair, and the plucky life which she led with her little daughter.

Lupin replied to none of my letters. I did not know whether they reached him; and, meantime, the date was drawing near and I could not help wondering whether his numerous undertakings would not prevent him from keeping the appointment which he himself had fixed.

As a matter of fact, the morning of the 15th of April arrived and Lupin was not with me by the time I had finished lunch. It was a quarter-past twelve. I left my flat and took a cab to Passy.

I had no sooner entered the lane than I saw the workman's four brats standing outside the door in the wall. Maître Valandier, informed by them of my arrival, hastened in my direction:

"Well?" he cried. "Where's Captain Jeanniot?"

"Hasn't he come?"

"No; and I can assure you that everybody is very impatient to see him."

The different groups began to crowd round the lawyer; and I noticed that all those faces which I recognized had thrown off the gloomy and despondent expression which they wore a year ago.

"They are full of hope," said Maître Valandier, "and it is my fault. But what could I do? Your friend made such an impression upon me that I spoke to these good people with a confidence... which I cannot say I feel. However, he seems a queer sort of fellow, this Captain Jeanniot of yours...."

He asked me many questions and I gave him a number of more or less fanciful details about the captain, to which the heirs listened, nodding their heads in appreciation of my remarks.

"Of course, the truth was bound to be discovered sooner or later," said the fat gentleman, in a tone of conviction.

The infantry corporal, dazzled by the captain's rank, did not entertain a doubt in his mind.

The lady with the little dog wanted to know if Captain Jeanniot was young.

But Louise d'Ernemont said:

"And suppose he does not come?"

"We shall still have the five thousand francs to divide," said the beggar-man.

For all that, Louise d'Ernemont's words had damped their enthusiasm. Their faces began to look sullen and I felt an atmosphere as of anguish weighing upon us.

At half-past one, the two lean sisters felt faint and sat down. Then the fat gentleman in the soiled suit suddenly rounded on the notary:

"It's you, Maître Valandier, who are to blame.... You ought to have brought the captain here by main force.... He's a humbug, that's quite clear."

He gave me a savage look, and the footman, in his turn, flung muttered curses at me.

I confess that their reproaches seemed to me well-founded and that Lupin's absence annoyed me greatly:

"He won't come now," I whispered to the lawyer.

And I was thinking of beating a retreat, when the eldest of the brats appeared at the door, yelling:

"There's someone coming!... A motorcycle!..."

A motor was throbbing on the other side of the wall. A man on a motor-bicycle came tearing down the lane at the risk of breaking his neck. Suddenly, he put on his brakes, outside the door, and sprang from his machine.

Under the layer of dust which covered him from head to foot, we could see that his navy-blue reefer-suit, his carefully creased trousers, his black felt hat and patent-leather boots were not the clothes in which a man usually goes cycling.

"But that's not Captain Jeanniot!" shouted the notary, who failed to recognize him.

"Yes, it is," said Lupin, shaking hands with us. "I'm Captain Jeanniot right enough... only I've shaved off my moustache.... Besides, Maître Valandier, here's your receipt."

He caught one of the workman's children by the arm and said:

"Run to the cab-rank and fetch a taxi to the corner of the Rue Raynouard. Look sharp! I have an urgent appointment to keep at two o'clock, or a quarter-past at the latest."

There was a murmur of protest. Captain Jeanniot took out his watch:

"Well! It's only twelve minutes to two! I have a good quarter of an hour before me. But, by Jingo, how tired I feel! And how hungry into the bargain!"

The corporal thrust his ammunition-bread into Lupin's hand; and he munched away at it as he sat down and said:

"You must forgive me. I was in the Marseilles express, which left the rails between Dijon and Laroche. There were twelve people killed and any number injured, whom I had to help. Then I found this motorcycle in the luggage-van.... Maître Valandier, you must be good enough to restore it to the owner. You will find the label fastened to the handlebar. Ah, you're back, my boy! Is the taxi there? At the corner of the Rue Raynouard? Capital!"

He looked at his watch again:

"Hullo! No time to lose!"

I stared at him with eager curiosity. But how great must the excitement of the d'Ernemont heirs have been! True, they had not the same faith in Captain Jeanniot that I had in Lupin. Nevertheless, their faces were pale and drawn. Captain Jeanniot turned slowly to the left and walked up to the sundial. The pedestal represented the figure of a man with a powerful torso, who bore on his shoulders a marble slab the surface of which had been so much worn by time that we could hardly distinguish the engraved lines that marked the hours. Above the slab, a Cupid, with outspread wings, held an arrow that served as a gnomon.

The captain stood leaning forward for a minute, with attentive eyes.

Then he said:

"Somebody lend me a knife, please."

A clock in the neighbourhood struck two. At that exact moment, the shadow of the arrow was thrown upon the sunlit dial along the line of a crack in the marble which divided the slab very nearly in half.

The captain took the knife handed to him. And with the point, very gently, he began to scratch the mixture of earth and moss that filled the narrow cleft.

Almost immediately, at a couple of inches from the edge, he stopped, as though his knife had encountered an obstacle, inserted his thumb and forefinger and withdrew a small object which he rubbed between the palms of his hands and gave to the lawyer:

"Here, Maître Valandier. Something to go on with."

It was an enormous diamond, the size of a hazelnut and beautifully cut.

The captain resumed his work. The next moment, a fresh stop. A second diamond, magnificent and brilliant as the first, appeared in sight.

And then came a third and a fourth.

In a minute's time, following the crack from one edge to the other and certainly without digging deeper than half an inch, the captain had taken out eighteen diamonds of the same size.

During this minute, there was not a cry, not a movement around the sundial. The heirs seemed paralyzed with a sort of stupor. Then the fat gentleman muttered:

"Geminy!"

And the corporal moaned:

"Oh, captain!... Oh, captain!..."

The two sisters fell in a dead faint. The lady with the little dog dropped on her knees and prayed, while the footman, staggering like a drunken man, held his head in his two hands, and Louise d'Ernemont wept.

When calm was restored and all became eager to thank Captain Jeanniot, they saw that he was gone.

Some years passed before I had an opportunity of talking to Lupin about this business. He was in a confidential vein and answered:

"The business of the eighteen diamonds? By Jove, when I think that three or four generations of my fellow-men had been hunting for the solution! And the eighteen diamonds were there all the time, under a little mud and dust!"

"But how did you guess?..."

"I did not guess. I reflected. I doubt if I need even have reflected. I was struck, from the beginning, by the fact that the whole circumstance was governed by one primary question: the question of time. When Charles d'Ernemont was still in possession of his wits, he wrote a date upon the three pictures. Later, in the gloom in which he was struggling, a faint glimmer of intelligence led him every year to the centre of the old garden; and the same faint glimmer led him away from it every year at the same moment, that is to say, at twenty-seven minutes past five. Something must have acted on the disordered machinery of his brain in this way. What was the superior force that controlled the poor madman's movements? Obviously, the instinctive notion of time represented by the sundial in the farmer-general's pictures. It was the annual revolution of the earth around the sun that brought Charles d'Ernemont back to the garden at a fixed date. And it was the earth's daily revolution upon its own axis that took him from it at a fixed hour, that is to say, at the hour, most likely, when the sun, concealed by objects different from those of today, ceased to light the Passy garden. Now of all this the sundial was the symbol. And that is why I at once knew where to look."

"But how did you settle the hour at which to begin looking?"

"Simply by the pictures. A man living at that time, such as Charles d'Ernemont, would have written either 26 Germinal, Year II, or else 15 April, 1794, but not 15 April, Year II. I was astounded that no one had thought of that."

"Then the figure 2 stood for two o'clock?"

"Evidently. And what must have happened was this: the farmer-general began by turning his fortune into solid gold and silver money. Then, by way of additional precaution, with this gold and silver he bought eighteen wonderful diamonds. When he was surprised by the arrival of the patrol, he fled into his garden. Which was the best place to hide the diamonds? Chance caused his eyes to light upon the sundial. It was two o'clock. The shadow of the arrow was then falling along the crack in the marble. He obeyed this sign of the shadow, rammed his eighteen diamonds into the dust and calmly went back and surrendered to the soldiers."

"But the shadow of the arrow coincides with the crack in the marble every day of the year and not only on the 15th of April."

40

"You forget, my dear chap, that we are dealing with a lunatic and that he remembered only this date of the 15th of April."

"Very well; but you, once you had solved the riddle, could easily have made your way into the enclosure and taken the diamonds."

"Quite true; and I should not have hesitated, if I had had to do with people of another description. But I really felt sorry for those poor wretches. And then you know the sort of idiot that Lupin is. The idea of appearing suddenly as a benevolent genius and amazing his kind would be enough to make him commit any sort of folly."

"Tah!" I cried. "The folly was not so great as all that. Six magnificent diamonds! How delighted the d'Ernemont heirs must have been to fulfil their part of the contract!"

Lupin looked at me and burst into uncontrollable laughter:

"So you haven't heard? Oh, what a joke! The delight of the d'Ernemont heirs!... Why, my dear fellow, on the next day, that worthy Captain Jenniot had so many mortal enemies! On the very next day, the two lean sisters and the fat gentleman organized an opposition. A contract? Not worth the paper it was written on, because, as could easily be proved, there was no such person as Captain Jenniot. Where did that adventurer spring from? Just let him sue them and they'd soon show him what was what!"

"Louise d'Ernemont too?"

"No, Louise d'Ernemont protested against that piece of rascality. But what could she do against so many? Besides, now that she was rich, she got back her young man. I haven't heard of her since."

"So...?"

"So, my dear fellow, I was caught in a trap, with not a leg to stand on, and I had to compromise and accept one modest diamond as my share, the smallest and the least handsome of the lot. That comes of doing one's best to help people!"

And Lupin grumbled between his teeth:

"Oh, gratitude!... All humbug!... Where should we honest men be if we had not our conscience and the satisfaction of duty performed to reward us?"

IV

THE INFERNAL TRAP

When the race was over, a crowd of people, streaming toward the exit from the grandstand, pushed against Nicolas Dugrival. He brought his hand smartly to the inside pocket of his jacket.

"What's the matter?" asked his wife.

"I still feel nervous... with that money on me! I'm afraid of some nasty accident."

She muttered:

"And I can't understand you. How can you think of carrying such a sum about with you? Every farthing we possess! Lord knows, it cost us trouble enough to earn!"

"Pooh!" he said. "No one would guess that it is here, in my pocketbook."

"Yes, yes," she grumbled. "That young manservant whom we discharged last week knew all about it, didn't he, Gabriel?"

"Yes, aunt," said a youth standing beside her.

Nicolas Dugrival, his wife and his nephew Gabriel were well-known figures at the race-meetings, where the regular frequenters saw them almost every day: Dugrival, a big, fat, red-faced man, who looked as if he knew how to enjoy life; his wife, also built on heavy lines, with a coarse, vulgar face, and always dressed in a plum-coloured silk much the worse for wear; the nephew, quite young, slender, with pale features, dark eyes and fair and rather curly hair.

As a rule, the couple remained seated throughout the afternoon. It was Gabriel who betted for his uncle, watching the horses in the paddock, picking up tips to right and left among the jockeys and stable-lads, running backward and forward between the stands and the parimutuel.

Luck had favoured them that day, for, three times, Dugrival's neighbours saw the young man come back and hand him money.

The fifth race was just finishing. Dugrival lit a cigar. At that moment, a gentleman in a tight-fitting brown suit, with a face ending in a peaked grey beard, came up to him and asked, in a confidential whisper:

"Does this happen to belong to you, sir?"

And he displayed a gold watch and chain.

Dugrival gave a start:

"Why, yes... it's mine.... Look, here are my initials, N. G.: Nicolas Dugrival!"

And he at once, with a movement of terror, clapped his hand to his jacket-pocket. The notecase was still there.

"Ah," he said, greatly relieved, "that's a piece of luck!... But, all the same, how on earth was it done?... Do you know the scoundrel?"

"Yes, we've got him locked up. Pray come with me and we'll soon look into the matter."

"Whom have I the honour…?"

"M. Delangle, detective-inspector. I have sent to let M. Marquenne, the magistrate, know."

Nicolas Dugrival went out with the inspector; and the two of them started for the commissary's office, some distance behind the grandstand. They were within fifty yards of it, when the inspector was accosted by a man who said to him, hurriedly:

"The fellow with the watch has blabbed; we are on the tracks of a whole gang. M. Marquenne wants you to wait for him at the parimutuel and to keep a lookout near the fourth booth."

There was a crowd outside the betting-booths and Inspector Delangle muttered:

"It's an absurd arrangement…. Whom am I to look out for?… That's just like M. Marquenne!…"

He pushed aside a group of people who were crowding too close upon him:

"By Jove, one has to use one's elbows here and keep a tight hold on one's purse. That's the way you got your watch pinched, M. Dugrival!"

"I can't understand…."

"Oh, if you knew how those gentry go to work! One never guesses what they're up to next. One of them treads on your foot, another gives you a poke in the eye with his stick and the third picks your pocket before you know where you are…. I've been had that way myself." He stopped and then continued, angrily. "But, bother it, what's the use of hanging about here! What a mob! It's unbearable!… Ah, there's M. Marquenne making signs to us!… One moment, please… and be sure and wait for me here."

He shouldered his way through the crowd. Nicolas Dugrival followed him for a moment with his eyes. Once the inspector was out of sight, he stood a little to one side, to avoid being hustled.

A few minutes passed. The sixth race was about to start, when Dugrival saw his wife and nephew looking for him. He explained to them that Inspector Delangle was arranging matters with the magistrate.

"Have you your money still?" asked his wife.

"Why, of course I have!" he replied. "The inspector and I took good care, I assure you, not to let the crowd jostle us."

He felt his jacket, gave a stifled cry, thrust his hand into his pocket and began to stammer inarticulate syllables, while Mme. Dugrival gasped, in dismay:

"What is it? What's the matter?"

"Stolen!" he moaned. "The pocketbook… the fifty notes!…"

"It's not true!" she screamed. "It's not true!"

"Yes, the inspector… a common sharper… he's the man…."

She uttered absolute yells:

"Thief! Thief! Stop thief!… My husband's been robbed!… Fifty thousand francs!… We are ruined!… Thief! Thief…"

In a moment they were surrounded by policemen and taken to the commissary's office. Dugrival went like a lamb, absolutely bewildered. His wife continued to shriek at the top of her voice, piling up explanations, railing against the inspector:

"Have him looked for!... Have him found!... A brown suit.... A pointed beard.... Oh, the villain, to think what he's robbed us of!... Fifty thousand francs!... Why... why, Dugrival, what are you doing?"

With one bound, she flung herself upon her husband. Too late! He had pressed the barrel of a revolver against his temple. A shot rang out. Dugrival fell. He was dead.

The reader cannot have forgotten the commotion made by the newspapers in connection with this case, nor how they jumped at the opportunity once more to accuse the police of carelessness and blundering. Was it conceivable that a pickpocket could play the part of an inspector like that, in broad daylight and in a public place, and rob a respectable man with impunity?

Nicolas Dugrival's widow kept the controversy alive, thanks to her jeremiads and to the interviews which she granted on every hand. A reporter had secured a snapshot of her in front of her husband's body, holding up her hand and swearing to revenge his death. Her nephew Gabriel was standing beside her, with hatred pictured in his face. He, too, it appeared, in a few words uttered in a whisper, but in a tone of fierce determination, had taken an oath to pursue and catch the murderer.

The accounts described the humble apartment which they occupied at the Batignolles; and, as they had been robbed of all their means, a sporting-paper opened a subscription on their behalf.

As for the mysterious Delangle, he remained undiscovered. Two men were arrested, but had to be released forthwith. The police took up a number of clues, which were at once abandoned; more than one name was mentioned; and, lastly, they accused Arsène Lupin, an action which provoked the famous burglar's celebrated cable, dispatched from New York six days after the incident:

"Protest indignantly against calumny invented by baffled police. Send my condolences to unhappy victims. Instructing my bankers to remit them fifty thousand francs.

"LUPIN."

True enough, on the day after the publication of the cable, a stranger rang at Mme. Dugrival's door and handed her an envelope. The envelope contained fifty thousand-franc notes.

This theatrical stroke was not at all calculated to allay the universal comment. But an event soon occurred which provided any amount of additional excitement. Two days later, the people living in the same house as Mme. Dugrival and her nephew were awakened, at four o'clock in the morning, by horrible cries and shrill calls for help. They rushed to the flat. The porter succeeded in opening the door. By the light of a lantern carried by one of the neighbours, he found Gabriel stretched at full-length in his bedroom, with his wrists and ankles bound and a gag forced into his mouth, while, in the next room, Mme. Dugrival lay with her life's blood ebbing away through a great gash in her breast.

She whispered:

"The money.... I've been robbed.... All the notes gone...."

44

And she fainted away.

What had happened? Gabriel said—and, as soon as she was able to speak, Mme. Dugrival completed her nephew's story—that he was startled from his sleep by finding himself attacked by two men, one of whom gagged him, while the other fastened him down. He was unable to see the men in the dark, but he heard the noise of the struggle between them and his aunt. It was a terrible struggle, Mme. Dugrival declared. The ruffians, who obviously knew their way about, guided by some intuition, made straight for the little cupboard containing the money and, in spite of her resistance and outcries, laid hands upon the bundle of banknotes. As they left, one of them, whom she had bitten in the arm, stabbed her with a knife, whereupon the men had both fled.

"Which way?" she was asked.

"Through the door of my bedroom and afterward, I suppose, through the hall-door."

"Impossible! The porter would have noticed them."

For the whole mystery lay in this: how had the ruffians entered the house and how did they manage to leave it? There was no outlet open to them. Was it one of the tenants? A careful inquiry proved the absurdity of such a supposition.

What then?

Chief-inspector Ganimard, who was placed in special charge of the case, confessed that he had never known anything more bewildering:

"It's very like Lupin," he said, "and yet it's not Lupin.... No, there's more in it than meets the eye, something very doubtful and suspicious.... Besides, if it were Lupin, why should he take back the fifty thousand francs which he sent? There's another question that puzzles me: what is the connection between the second robbery and the first, the one on the racecourse? The whole thing is incomprehensible and I have a sort of feeling—which is very rare with me—that it is no use hunting. For my part, I give it up."

The examining-magistrate threw himself into the case with heart and soul. The reporters united their efforts with those of the police. A famous English sleuthhound crossed the Channel. A wealthy American, whose head had been turned by detective-stories, offered a big reward to whosoever should supply the first information leading to the discovery of the truth. Six weeks later, no one was any the wiser. The public adopted Ganimard's view; and the examining-magistrate himself grew tired of struggling in a darkness which only became denser as time went on.

And life continued as usual with Dugrival's widow. Nursed by her nephew, she soon recovered from her wound. In the mornings, Gabriel settled her in an easy-chair at the dining-room window, did the rooms and then went out marketing. He cooked their lunch without even accepting the proffered assistance of the porter's wife.

Worried by the police investigations and especially by the requests for interviews, the aunt and nephew refused to see anybody. Not even the portress, whose chatter disturbed and wearied Mme. Dugrival, was admitted. She fell back upon Gabriel, whom she accosted each time that he passed her room:

"Take care, M. Gabriel, you're both of you being spied upon. There are men watching you. Why, only last night, my husband caught a fellow staring up at your windows."

"Nonsense!" said Gabriel. "It's all right. That's the police, protecting us."

One afternoon, at about four o'clock, there was a violent altercation between two costermongers at the bottom of the street. The porter's wife at once left her room to listen to the invectives which the adversaries were hurling at each other's heads. Her back was no sooner turned than a man, young, of medium height and dressed in a grey suit of irreproachable cut, slipped into the house and ran up the staircase.

When he came to the third floor, he rang the bell. Receiving no answer, he rang again. At the third summons, the door opened.

"Mme. Dugrival?" he asked, taking off his hat.

"Mme. Dugrival is still an invalid and unable to see anyone," said Gabriel, who stood in the hall.

"It's most important that I should speak to her."

"I am her nephew and perhaps I could take her a message...."

"Very well," said the man. "Please tell Mme. Dugrival that an accident has supplied me with valuable information concerning the robbery from which she has suffered and that I should like to go over the flat and ascertain certain particulars for myself. I am accustomed to this sort of inquiry; and my call is sure to be of use to her."

Gabriel examined the visitor for a moment, reflected and said:

"In that case, I suppose my aunt will consent... Pray come in."

He opened the door of the dining-room and stepped back to allow the other to pass. The stranger walked to the threshold, but, at the moment when he was crossing it, Gabriel raised his arm and, with a swift movement, struck him with a dagger over the right shoulder.

A burst of laughter rang through the room:

"Got him!" cried Mme. Dugrival, darting up from her chair. "Well done, Gabriel! But, I say, you haven't killed the scoundrel, have you?"

"I don't think so, aunt. It's a small blade and I didn't strike him too hard."

The man was staggering, with his hands stretched in front of him and his face deathly pale.

"You fool!" sneered the widow. "So you've fallen into the trap... and a good job too! We've been looking out for you a long time. Come, my fine fellow, down with you! You don't care about it, do you? But you can't help yourself, you see. That's right: one knee on the ground, before the missus... now the other knee.... How well we've been brought up!... Crash, there we go on the floor! Lord, if my poor Dugrival could only see him like that!... And now, Gabriel, to work!"

She went to her bedroom and opened one of the doors of a hanging wardrobe filled with dresses. Pulling these aside, she pushed open another door which formed the back of the wardrobe and led to a room in the next house:

"Help me carry him, Gabriel. And you'll nurse him as well as you can, won't you? For the present, he's worth his weight in gold to us, the artist!..."

The hours succeeded one another. Days passed.

One morning, the wounded man regained a moment's consciousness. He raised his eyelids and looked around him.

He was lying in a room larger than that in which he had been stabbed, a room sparsely furnished, with thick curtains hanging before the windows from top to bottom. There was light enough, however, to enable him to see young Gabriel Dugrival seated on a chair beside him and watching him.

"Ah, it's you, youngster!" he murmured. "I congratulate you, my lad. You have a sure and pretty touch with the dagger."

And he fell asleep again.

That day and the following days, he woke up several times and, each time, he saw the stripling's pale face, his thin lips and his dark eyes, with the hard look in them:

"You frighten me," he said. "If you have sworn to do for me, don't stand on ceremony. But cheer up, for goodness' sake. The thought of death has always struck me as the most humorous thing in the world. Whereas, with you, old chap, it simply becomes lugubrious. I prefer to go to sleep. Good night!"

Still, Gabriel, in obedience to Mme. Dugrival's orders, continued to nurse him with the utmost care and attention. The patient was almost free from fever and was beginning to take beef-tea and milk. He gained a little strength and jested:

"When will the convalescent be allowed his first drive? Is the bath-chair there? Why, cheer up, stupid! You look like a weeping-willow contemplating a crime. Come, just one little smile for daddy!"

One day, on waking, he had a very unpleasant feeling of constraint. After a few efforts, he perceived that, during his sleep, his legs, chest and arms had been fastened to the bedstead with thin wire strands that cut into his flesh at the least movements.

"Ah," he said to his keeper, "this time it's the great performance! The chicken's going to be bled. Are you operating, Angel Gabriel? If so, see that your razor's nice and clean, old chap! The antiseptic treatment, *if* you please!"

But he was interrupted by the sound of a key grating in the lock. The door opposite opened and Mme. Dugrival appeared.

She approached slowly, took a chair and, producing a revolver from her pocket, cocked it and laid it on the table by the bedside.

"*Brrrrr!*" said the prisoner. "We might be at the Ambigu!... Fourth act: the Traitor's Doom. And the fair sex to do the deed.... The hand of the Graces.... What an honour!... Mme. Dugrival, I rely on you not to disfigure me."

"Hold your tongue, Lupin."

"Ah, so you know?... By Jove, how clever we are!"

"Hold your tongue, Lupin."

There was a solemn note in her voice that impressed the captive and compelled him to silence. He watched his two gaolers in turns. The bloated features and red complexion of Mme. Dugrival formed a striking contrast with her nephew's refined face; but they both wore the same air of implacable resolve.

The widow leant forward and said:

"Are you prepared to answer my questions?"

"Why not?"

"Then listen to me. How did you know that Dugrival carried all his money in his pocket?"

"Servants' gossip...."

"A young manservant whom we had in our employ: was that it?"

"Yes."

"And did you steal Dugrival's watch in order to give it back to him and inspire him with confidence?"

"Yes."

She suppressed a movement of fury:

"You fool! You fool!... What! You rob my man, you drive him to kill himself and, instead of making tracks to the uttermost ends of the earth and hiding yourself, you go on playing Lupin in the heart of Paris!... Did you forget that I swore, on my dead husband's head, to find his murderer?"

"That's what staggers me," said Lupin. "How did you come to suspect me?"

"How? Why, you gave yourself away!"

"I did?..."

"Of course.... The fifty thousand francs...."

"Well, what about it? A present...."

"Yes, a present which you gave cabled instructions to have sent to me, so as to make believe that you were in America on the day of the races. A present, indeed! What humbug! The fact is, you didn't like to think of the poor fellow whom you had murdered. So you restored the money to the widow, publicly, of course, because you love playing to the gallery and ranting and posing, like the mountebank that you are. That was all very nicely thought out. Only, my fine fellow, you ought not to have sent me the selfsame notes that were stolen from Dugrival! Yes, you silly fool, the selfsame notes and no others! We knew the numbers, Dugrival and I did. And you were stupid enough to send the bundle to me. Now do you understand your folly?"

Lupin began to laugh:

"It was a pretty blunder, I confess. I'm not responsible; I gave different orders. But, all the same I can't blame anyone except myself."

"Ah, so you admit it! You signed your theft and you signed your ruin at the same time. There was nothing left to be done but to find you. Find you? No, better than that. Sensible people don't find Lupin: they make him come to them! That was a masterly notion. It belongs to my young nephew, who loathes you as much as I do, if possible, and who knows you thoroughly, through reading all the books that have been written about you. He knows your prying nature, your need to be always plotting, your mania for hunting in the dark and unravelling what others have failed to unravel. He also knows that sort of sham kindness of yours, the drivelling sentimentality that makes you shed crocodile tears over the people you victimize; And he planned the whole farce! He invented the story of the two burglars, the second theft of fifty thousand francs! Oh, I swear to you, before Heaven, that the stab which I gave myself with my own hands never hurt me! And I swear to you, before Heaven, that we spent a glorious time waiting for you, the boy and I, peeping out at your confederates who prowled under our windows, taking their bearings! And there was no mistake about it: you were bound to come! Seeing that you had restored the Widow Dugrival's fifty thousand francs, it was out of the question that you should allow the Widow Dugrival to be robbed of her fifty thousand francs! You were bound to come, attracted by the scent of the mystery. You were bound to come, for swagger, out of vanity! And you come!"

The widow gave a strident laugh:

"Well played, wasn't it? The Lupin of Lupins, the master of masters, inaccessible and invisible, caught in a trap by a woman and a boy!... Here he is in flesh and bone... here he is with hands and feet tied, no more dangerous than a sparrow... here is he... here he is!..."

She shook with joy and began to pace the room, throwing sidelong glances at the bed, like a wild beast that does not for a moment take its eyes from its victim. And never had Lupin beheld greater hatred and savagery in any human being.

"Enough of this prattle," she said.

Suddenly restraining herself, she stalked back to him and, in a quite different tone, in a hollow voice, laying stress on every syllable:

"Thanks to the papers in your pocket, Lupin, I have made good use of the last twelve days. I know all your affairs, all your schemes, all your assumed names, all the organization of your band, all the lodgings which you possess in Paris and elsewhere. I have even visited one of them, the most secret, the one where you hide your papers, your ledgers and the whole story of your financial operations. The result of my investigations is very satisfactory. Here are four cheques, taken from four chequebooks and corresponding with four accounts which you keep at four different banks under four different names. I have filled in each of them for ten thousand francs. A larger figure would have been too risky. And, now, sign."

"By Jove!" said Lupin, sarcastically. "This is blackmail, my worthy Mme. Dugrival."

"That takes your breath away, what?"

"It takes my breath away, as you say."

"And you find an adversary who is a match for you?"

"The adversary is far beyond me. So the trap—let us call it infernal—the infernal trap into which I have fallen was laid not merely by a widow thirsting for revenge, but also by a first-rate business woman anxious to increase her capital?"

"Just so."

"My congratulations. And, while I think of it, used M. Dugrival perhaps to...?"

"You have hit it, Lupin. After all, why conceal the fact? It will relieve your conscience. Yes, Lupin, Dugrival used to work on the same lines as yourself. Oh, not on the same scale!... We were modest people: a louis here, a louis there... a purse or two which we trained Gabriel to pick up at the races.... And, in this way, we had made our little pile... just enough to buy a small place in the country."

"I prefer it that way," said Lupin.

"That's all right! I'm only telling you, so that you may know that I am not a beginner and that you have nothing to hope for. A rescue? No. The room in which we now are communicates with my bedroom. It has a private outlet of which nobody knows. It was Dugrival's special apartment. He used to see his friends here. He kept his implements and tools here, his disguises... his telephone even, as you perceive. So there's no hope, you see. Your accomplices have given up looking for you here. I have sent them off on another track. Your goose is cooked. Do you begin to realize the position?"

"Yes."

"Then sign the cheques."

"And, when I have signed them, shall I be free?"

"I must cash them first."

"And after that?"

"After that, on my soul, as I hope to be saved, you will be free."

"I don't trust you."

"Have you any choice?"

"That's true. Hand me the cheques."

She unfastened Lupin's right hand, gave him a pen and said:

"Don't forget that the four cheques require four different signatures and that the handwriting has to be altered in each case."

"Never fear."

He signed the cheques.

"Gabriel," said the widow, "it is ten o'clock. If I am not back by twelve, it will mean that this scoundrel has played me one of his tricks. At twelve o'clock, blow out his brains. I am leaving you the revolver with which your uncle shot himself. There are five bullets left out of the six. That will be ample."

She left the room, humming a tune as she went.

Lupin mumbled:

"I wouldn't give twopence for my life."

He shut his eyes for an instant and then, suddenly, said to Gabriel:

"How much?"

And, when the other did not appear to understand, he grew irritated:

"I mean what I say. How much? Answer me, can't you? We drive the same trade, you and I. I steal, thou stealest, we steal. So we ought to come to terms: that's what we are here for. Well? Is it a bargain? Shall we clear out together. I will give you a post in my gang, an easy, well-paid post. How much do you want for yourself? Ten thousand? Twenty thousand? Fix your own price; don't be shy. There's plenty to be had for the asking."

An angry shiver passed through his frame as he saw the impassive face of his keeper:

"Oh, the beggar won't even answer! Why, you can't have been so fond of old Dugrival as all that! Listen to me: if you consent to release me...."

But he interrupted himself. The young man's eyes wore the cruel expression which he knew so well. What was the use of trying to move him?

"Hang it all!" he snarled. "I'm not going to croak here, like a dog! Oh, if I could only...."

Stiffening all his muscles, he tried to burst his bonds, making a violent effort that drew a cry of pain from him; and he fell back upon his bed, exhausted.

"Well, well," he muttered, after a moment, "it's as the widow said: my goose is cooked. Nothing to be done. *De profundis*, Lupin."

A quarter of an hour passed, half an hour....

Gabriel, moving closer to Lupin, saw that his eyes were shut and that his breath came evenly, like that of a man sleeping. But Lupin said:

"Don't imagine that I'm asleep, youngster. No, people don't sleep at a moment like this. Only I am consoling myself. Needs must, eh?... And then I am thinking of what is to come after.... Exactly. I have a little theory of my own about that. You wouldn't think it, to look at me, but I believe in metempsychosis, in the transmigration of souls. It would take too long to explain, however.... I say, boy... suppose we shook hands before we part? You won't? Then goodbye. Good health and a long life to you, Gabriel!..."

He closed his eyelids and did not stir again before Mme. Dugrival's return.

The widow entered with a lively step, at a few minutes before twelve. She seemed greatly excited:

"I have the money," she said to her nephew. "Run away. I'll join you in the motor down below."

"But...."

"I don't want your help to finish him off. I can do that alone. Still, if you feel like seeing the sort of a face a rogue can pull.... Pass me the weapon."

Gabriel handed her the revolver and the widow continued:

"Have you burnt our papers?"

"Yes."

"Then to work. And, as soon as he's done for, be off. The shots may bring the neighbours. They must find both the flats empty."

She went up to the bed:

"Are you ready, Lupin?"

"Ready's not the word: I'm burning with impatience."

"Have you any request to make of me?"

"None."

"Then...."

"One word, though."

"What is it?"

"If I meet Dugrival in the next world, what message am I to give him from you?"

She shrugged her shoulders and put the barrel of the revolver to Lupin's temple.

"That's it," he said, "and be sure your hand doesn't shake, my dear lady. It won't hurt you, I swear. Are you ready? At the word of command, eh? One... two... three...."

The widow pulled the trigger. A shot rang out.

"Is this death?" said Lupin. "That's funny! I should have thought it was something much more different from life!"

There was a second shot. Gabriel snatched the weapon from his aunt's hands and examined it:

"Ah," he exclaimed, "the bullets have been removed!... There are only the percussion-caps left!..."

His aunt and he stood motionless, for a moment, and confused:

"Impossible!" she blurted out. "Who could have done it?... An inspector?... The examining-magistrate?..."

She stopped and, in a low voice:

"Hark.... I hear a noise...."

They listened and the widow went into the hall. She returned, furious, exasperated by her failure and by the scare which she had received:

"There's nobody there.... It must have been the neighbours going out.... We have plenty of time.... Ah, Lupin, you were beginning to make merry!... The knife, Gabriel."

"It's in my room."

"Go and fetch it."

Gabriel hurried away. The widow stamped with rage:

"I've sworn to do it!... You've got to suffer, my fine fellow!... I swore to Dugrival that I would do it and I have repeated my oath every morning and evening since.... I have taken it on my knees, yes, on my knees, before Heaven that listens to me! It's my duty and my right to revenge my dead husband!... By the way, Lupin, you don't look quite as merry as you did!... Lord, one would almost think you were afraid!... He's afraid! He's afraid! I can see it in his eyes!... Come along, Gabriel, my boy!... Look at his eyes!... Look at his lips!... He's trembling!... Give me the knife, so that I may dig it into his heart while he's shivering.... Oh, you coward!... Quick, quick, Gabriel, the knife!..."

"I can't find it anywhere," said the young man, running back in dismay. "It has gone from my room! I can't make it out!"

"Never mind!" cried the Widow Dugrival, half demented. "All the better! I will do the business myself."

She seized Lupin by the throat, clutched him with her ten fingers, digging her nails into his flesh, and began to squeeze with all her might. Lupin uttered a hoarse rattle and gave himself up for lost.

Suddenly, there was a crash at the window. One of the panes was smashed to pieces.

"What's that? What is it?" stammered the widow, drawing herself erect, in alarm.

Gabriel, who had turned even paler than usual, murmured:

"I don't know.... I can't think...."

"Who can have done it?" said the widow.

She dared not move, waiting for what would come next. And one thing above all terrified her, the fact that there was no missile on the floor around them, although the pane of glass, as was clearly visible, had given way before the crash of a heavy and fairly large object, a stone, probably.

After a while, she looked under the bed, under the chest of drawers:

"Nothing," she said.

"No," said her nephew, who was also looking. And, resuming her seat, she said:

"I feel frightened... my arms fail me... you finish him off...."

Gabriel confessed:

"I'm frightened also."

"Still... still," she stammered, "it's got to be done.... I swore it...."

Making one last effort, she returned to Lupin and gasped his neck with her stiff fingers. But Lupin, who was watching her pallid face, received a very clear sensation that she would not have the courage to kill him. To her he was becoming something sacred, invulnerable. A mysterious power was protecting him against every attack, a power which had already saved him three times by inexplicable means and which would find other means to protect him against the wiles of death.

She said to him, in a hoarse voice:

"How you must be laughing at me!"

"Not at all, upon my word. I should feel frightened myself, in your place."

"Nonsense, you scum of the earth! You imagine that you will be rescued... that your friends are waiting outside? It's out of the question, my fine fellow."

"I know. It's not they defending me... nobody's defending me...."

"Well, then?..."

"Well, all the same, there's something strange at the bottom of it, something fantastic and miraculous that makes your flesh creep, my fine lady."

"You villain!... You'll be laughing on the other side of your mouth before long."

"I doubt it."

"You wait and see."

She reflected once more and said to her nephew:

"What would you do?"

"Fasten his arm again and let's be off," he replied.

A hideous suggestion! It meant condemning Lupin to the most horrible of all deaths, death by starvation.

"No," said the widow. "He might still find a means of escape. I know something better than that."

She took down the receiver of the telephone, waited and asked:

"Number 82248, please."

And, after a second or two:

"Hullo!... Is that the Criminal Investigation Department?... Is Chief-inspector Ganimard there?... In twenty minutes, you say?... I'm sorry!... However!... When he comes, give him this message from Mme. Dugrival.... Yes, Mme. Nicolas Dugrival.... Ask him to come to my flat. Tell him to open the looking-glass door of my wardrobe; and, when he has done so, he will see that the wardrobe hides an outlet which makes my bedroom communicate with two other rooms. In one of these, he will find a man bound hand and foot. It is the thief, Dugrival's murderer.... You don't believe me?... Tell M. Ganimard; he'll believe me right enough.... Oh, I was almost forgetting to give you the man's name: Arsène Lupin!"

And, without another word, she replaced the receiver.

"There, Lupin, that's done. After all, I would just as soon have my revenge this way. How I shall hold my sides when I read the reports of the Lupin trial!... Are you coming, Gabriel?"

"Yes, aunt."

"Goodbye, Lupin. You and I shan't see each other again, I expect, for we are going abroad. But I promise to send you some sweets while you're in prison."

"Chocolates, mother! We'll eat them together!"

"Goodbye."

"Au revoir."

The widow went out with her nephew, leaving Lupin fastened down to the bed.

He at once moved his free arm and tried to release himself; but he realized, at the first attempt, that he would never have the strength to break the wire strands that bound him. Exhausted with fever and pain, what could he do in the twenty minutes or so that were left to him before Ganimard's arrival?

Nor did he count upon his friends. True, he had been thrice saved from death; but this was evidently due to an astounding series of accidents and not to any interference on the part of his allies. Otherwise they would not have contented themselves with these extraordinary manifestations, but would have rescued him for good and all.

No, he must abandon all hope. Ganimard was coming. Ganimard would find him there. It was inevitable. There was no getting away from the fact.

And the prospect of what was coming irritated him singularly. He already heard his old enemy's gibes ringing in his ears. He foresaw the roars of laughter with which the incredible news would be greeted on the morrow. To be arrested in action, so to speak, on the battlefield, by an imposing detachment of adversaries, was one thing: but to be arrested, or rather picked up, scraped up, gathered up, in such condition, was really too silly. And Lupin, who had so often scoffed at others, felt all the ridicule that was falling to his share in this ending of the Dugrival business, all the bathos of allowing himself to be caught in the widow's infernal trap and finally of being "served up" to the police like a dish of game, roasted to a turn and nicely seasoned.

"Blow the widow!" he growled. "I had rather she had cut my throat and done with it."

He pricked up his ears. Someone was moving in the next room. Ganimard! No. Great as his eagerness would be, he could not be there yet. Besides, Ganimard would not have acted like that, would not have opened the door as gently as that other person was doing. What other person? Lupin remembered the three miraculous interventions to which he owed his life. Was it possible that there was really somebody who had protected him against the widow, and that that somebody was now attempting to rescue him? But, if so, who?

Unseen by Lupin, the stranger stooped behind the bed. Lupin heard the sound of the pliers attacking the wire strands and releasing him little by little. First his chest was freed, then his arms, then his legs.

And a voice said to him:

"You must get up and dress."

Feeling very weak, he half-raised himself in bed at the moment when the stranger rose from her stooping posture.

"Who are you?" he whispered. "Who are you?"

And a great surprise over came him.

By his side stood a woman, a woman dressed in black, with a lace shawl over her head, covering part of her face. And the woman, as far as he could judge, was young and of a graceful and slender stature.

"Who are you?" he repeated.

"You must come now," said the woman. "There's no time to lose."

"Can I?" asked Lupin, making a desperate effort. "I doubt if I have the strength."

"Drink this."

She poured some milk into a cup; and, as she handed it to him, her lace opened, leaving the face uncovered.

"You!" he stammered. "It's you!... It's you who... it was you who were...."

He stared in amazement at this woman whose features presented so striking a resemblance to Gabriel's, whose delicate, regular face had the same pallor, whose mouth wore the same hard and forbidding expression. No sister could have borne so great a likeness to her brother. There was not a doubt possible: it was the identical person. And, without believing for a moment that Gabriel had concealed himself in a woman's clothes, Lupin, on the contrary, received the distinct impression that it was a woman standing beside him and that the stripling who had pursued him with his hatred and struck him

54

with the dagger was in very deed a woman. In order to follow their trade with greater ease, the Dugrival pair had accustomed her to disguise herself as a boy.

"You... you...!" he repeated. "Who would have suspected...?"

She emptied the contents of a phial into the cup:

"Drink this cordial," she said.

He hesitated, thinking of poison.

She added:

"It was I who saved you."

"Of course, of course," he said. "It was you who removed the bullets from the revolver?"

"Yes."

"And you who hid the knife?"

"Here it is, in my pocket."

"And you who smashed the windowpane while your aunt was throttling me?"

"Yes, it was I, with the paperweight on the table: I threw it into the street."

"But why? Why?" he asked, in utter amazement.

"Drink the cordial."

"Didn't you want me to die? But then why did you stab me to begin with?"

"Drink the cordial."

He emptied the cup at a draught, without quite knowing the reason of his sudden confidence.

"Dress yourself... quickly," she commanded, retiring to the window.

He obeyed and she came back to him, for he had dropped into a chair, exhausted.

"We must go now, we must, we have only just time.... Collect your strength."

She bent forward a little, so that he might lean on her shoulder, and turned toward the door and the staircase.

And Lupin walked as one walks in a dream, one of those queer dreams in which the most inconsequent things occur, a dream that was the happy sequel of the terrible nightmare in which he had lived for the past fortnight.

A thought struck him, however. He began to laugh:

"Poor Ganimard! Upon my word, the fellow has no luck, I would give twopence to see him coming to arrest me."

After descending the staircase with the aid of his companion, who supported him with incredible vigour, he found himself in the street, opposite a motorcar into which she helped him to mount.

"Right away," she said to the driver.

Lupin, dazed by the open air and the speed at which they were travelling, hardly took stock of the drive and of the incidents on the road. He recovered all his consciousness when he found himself at home in one of the flats which he occupied, looked after by his servant, to whom the girl gave a few rapid instructions.

"You can go," he said to the man.

But, when the girl turned to go as well, he held her back by a fold of her dress.

"No... no... you must first explain.... Why did you save me? Did you return unknown to your aunt? But why did you save me? Was it from pity?"

55

She did not answer. With her figure drawn up and her head flung back a little, she retained her hard and impenetrable air. Nevertheless, he thought he noticed that the lines of her mouth showed not so much cruelty as bitterness. Her eyes, her beautiful dark eyes, revealed melancholy. And Lupin, without as yet understanding, received a vague intuition of what was passing within her. He seized her hand. She pushed him away, with a start of revolt in which he felt hatred, almost repulsion. And, when he insisted, she cried:

"Let me be, will you?... Let me be!... Can't you see that I detest you?"

They looked at each other for a moment, Lupin disconcerted, she quivering and full of uneasiness, her pale face all flushed with unwonted colour.

He said to her, gently:

"If you detested me, you should have let me die.... It was simple enough.... Why didn't you?"

"Why?... Why?... How do I know?..."

Her face contracted. With a sudden movement, she hid it in her two hands; and he saw tears trickle between her fingers.

Greatly touched, he thought of addressing her in fond words, such as one would use to a little girl whom one wished to console, and of giving her good advice and saving her, in his turn, and snatching her from the bad life which she was leading, perhaps against her better nature.

But such words would have sounded ridiculous, coming from his lips, and he did not know what to say, now that he understood the whole story and was able to picture the young woman sitting beside his sickbed, nursing the man whom she had wounded, admiring his pluck and gaiety, becoming attached to him, falling in love with him and thrice over, probably in spite of herself, under a sort of instinctive impulse, amid fits of spite and rage, saving him from death.

And all this was so strange, so unforeseen; Lupin was so much unmanned by his astonishment, that, this time, he did not try to retain her when she made for the door, backward, without taking her eyes from him.

She lowered her head, smiled for an instant and disappeared.

He rang the bell, quickly:

"Follow that woman," he said to his man. "Or no, stay where you are.... After all, it is better so...."

He sat brooding for a while, possessed by the girl's image. Then he revolved in his mind all that curious, stirring and tragic adventure, in which he had been so very near succumbing; and, taking a hand-glass from the table, he gazed for a long time and with a certain self-complacency at his features, which illness and pain had not succeeded in impairing to any great extent:

"Good looks count for something, after all!" he muttered.

V

THE RED SILK SCARF

On leaving his house one morning, at his usual early hour for going to the Law Courts, Chief-inspector Ganimard noticed the curious behaviour of an individual who was walking along the Rue Pergolèse in front of him. Shabbily dressed and wearing a straw hat, though the day was the first of December, the man stooped at every thirty or forty yards to fasten his bootlace, or pick up his stick, or for some other reason. And, each time, he took a little piece of orange-peel from his pocket and laid it stealthily on the kerb of the pavement. It was probably a mere display of eccentricity, a childish amusement to which no one else would have paid attention; but Ganimard was one of those shrewd observers who are indifferent to nothing that strikes their eyes and who are never satisfied until they know the secret cause of things. He therefore began to follow the man.

Now, at the moment when the fellow was turning to the right, into the Avenue de la Grande-Armée, the inspector caught him exchanging signals with a boy of twelve or thirteen, who was walking along the houses on the left-hand side. Twenty yards farther, the man stooped and turned up the bottom of his trousers legs. A bit of orange-peel marked the place. At the same moment, the boy stopped and, with a piece of chalk, drew a white cross, surrounded by a circle, on the wall of the house next to him.

The two continued on their way. A minute later, a fresh halt. The strange individual picked up a pin and dropped a piece of orange-peel; and the boy at once made a second cross on the wall and again drew a white circle round it.

"By Jove!" thought the chief-inspector, with a grunt of satisfaction. "This is rather promising.... What on earth can those two merchants be plotting?"

The two "merchants" went down the Avenue Friedland and the Rue du Faubourg-Saint-Honoré, but nothing occurred that was worthy of special mention. The double performance was repeated at almost regular intervals and, so to speak, mechanically. Nevertheless, it was obvious, on the one hand, that the man with the orange-peel did not do his part of the business until after he had picked out with a glance the house that was to be marked and, on the other hand, that the boy did not mark that particular house until after he had observed his companion's signal. It was certain, therefore, that there was an agreement between the two; and the proceedings presented no small interest in the chief-inspector's eyes.

At the Place Beauveau the man hesitated. Then, apparently making up his mind, he twice turned up and twice turned down the bottom of his trousers legs. Hereupon, the boy sat down on the kerb, opposite the sentry who was mounting guard outside the Ministry of the Interior, and marked the flagstone with two little crosses contained within two circles. The same ceremony was gone through a little further on, when they reached the Élysée. Only, on the pavement where the President's sentry was marching up and down, there were three signs instead of two.

"Hang it all!" muttered Ganimard, pale with excitement and thinking, in spite of himself, of his inveterate enemy, Lupin, whose name came to his mind whenever a mysterious circumstance presented itself. "Hang it all, what does it mean?"

He was nearly collaring and questioning the two "merchants." But he was too clever to commit so gross a blunder. The man with the orange-peel had now lit a cigarette; and the boy, also placing a cigarette-end between his lips, had gone up to him, apparently with the object of asking for a light.

They exchanged a few words. Quick as thought, the boy handed his companion an object which looked—at least, so the inspector believed—like a revolver. They both bent over this object; and the man, standing with his face to the wall, put his hand six times in his pocket and made a movement as though he were loading a weapon.

As soon as this was done, they walked briskly to the Rue de Surène; and the inspector, who followed them as closely as he was able to do without attracting their attention, saw them enter the gateway of an old house of which all the shutters were closed, with the exception of those on the third or top floor.

He hurried in after them. At the end of the carriage-entrance he saw a large courtyard, with a house-painter's sign at the back and a staircase on the left.

He went up the stairs and, as soon as he reached the first floor, ran still faster, because he heard, right up at the top, a din as of a free-fight.

When he came to the last landing he found the door open. He entered, listened for a second, caught the sound of a struggle, rushed to the room from which the sound appeared to proceed and remained standing on the threshold, very much out of breath and greatly surprised to see the man of the orange-peel and the boy banging the floor with chairs.

At that moment a third person walked out of an adjoining room. It was a young man of twenty-eight or thirty, wearing a pair of short whiskers in addition to his moustache, spectacles, and a smoking-jacket with an astrakhan collar and looking like a foreigner, a Russian.

"Good morning, Ganimard," he said. And turning to the two companions, "Thank you, my friends, and all my congratulations on the successful result. Here's the reward I promised you."

He gave them a hundred-franc note, pushed them outside and shut both doors.

"I am sorry, old chap," he said to Ganimard. "I wanted to talk to you… wanted to talk to you badly."

He offered him his hand and, seeing that the inspector remained flabbergasted and that his face was still distorted with anger, he exclaimed:

"Why, you don't seem to understand!… And yet it's clear enough…. I wanted to see you particularly…. So what could I do?" And, pretending to reply to an objection, "No, no, old chap," he continued. "You're quite wrong. If I had written or telephoned, you would not have come… or else you would have come with a regiment. Now I wanted to see you all alone; and I thought the best thing was to send those two decent fellows to meet you, with orders to scatter bits of orange-peel and draw crosses and circles, in short, to mark out your road to this place…. Why, you look quite bewildered! What is it? Perhaps you don't recognize me? Lupin…. Arsène Lupin…. Ransack your memory…. Doesn't the name remind you of anything?"

"You dirty scoundrel!" Ganimard snarled between his teeth.

Lupin seemed greatly distressed and, in an affectionate voice:

"Are you vexed? Yes, I can see it in your eyes.... The Dugrival business, I suppose? I ought to have waited for you to come and take me in charge?... There now, the thought never occurred to me! I promise you, next time...."

"You scum of the earth!" growled Ganimard.

"And I thinking I was giving you a treat! Upon my word, I did. I said to myself, 'That dear old Ganimard! We haven't met for an age. He'll simply rush at me when he sees me!'"

Ganimard, who had not yet stirred a limb, seemed to be waking from his stupor. He looked around him, looked at Lupin, visibly asked himself whether he would not do well to rush at him in reality and then, controlling himself, took hold of a chair and settled himself in it, as though he had suddenly made up his mind to listen to his enemy:

"Speak," he said. "And don't waste my time with any nonsense. I'm in a hurry."

"That's it," said Lupin, "let's talk. You can't imagine a quieter place than this. It's an old manor-house, which once stood in the open country, and it belongs to the Duc de Rochelaure. The duke, who has never lived in it, lets this floor to me and the outhouses to a painter and decorator. I always keep up a few establishments of this kind: it's a sound, practical plan. Here, in spite of my looking like a Russian nobleman, I am M. Daubreuil, an ex-cabinet-minister.... You understand, I had to select a rather overstocked profession, so as not to attract attention...."

"Do you think I care a hang about all this?" said Ganimard, interrupting him.

"Quite right, I'm wasting words and you're in a hurry. Forgive me. I shan't be long now.... Five minutes, that's all.... I'll start at once.... Have a cigar? No? Very well, no more will I."

He sat down also, drummed his fingers on the table, while thinking, and began in this fashion:

"On the 17th of October, 1599, on a warm and sunny autumn day... Do you follow me?... But, now that I come to think of it, is it really necessary to go back to the reign of Henry IV, and tell you all about the building of the Pont-Neuf? No, I don't suppose you are very well up in French history; and I should only end by muddling you. Suffice it, then, for you to know that, last night, at one o'clock in the morning, a boatman passing under the last arch of the Pont-Neuf aforesaid, along the left bank of the river, heard something drop into the front part of his barge. The thing had been flung from the bridge and its evident destination was the bottom of the Seine. The bargee's dog rushed forward, barking, and, when the man reached the end of his craft, he saw the animal worrying a piece of newspaper that had served to wrap up a number of objects. He took from the dog such of the contents as had not fallen into the water, went to his cabin and examined them carefully. The result struck him as interesting; and, as the man is connected with one of my friends, he sent to let me know. This morning I was waked up and placed in possession of the facts and of the objects which the man had collected. Here they are."

He pointed to them, spread out on a table. There were, first of all, the torn pieces of a newspaper. Next came a large cut-glass inkstand, with a long piece of string fastened to the lid. There was a bit of broken glass and a sort of flexible cardboard, reduced to

59

shreds. Lastly, there was a piece of bright scarlet silk, ending in a tassel of the same material and colour.

"You see our exhibits, friend of my youth," said Lupin. "No doubt, the problem would be more easily solved if we had the other objects which went overboard owing to the stupidity of the dog. But it seems to me, all the same, that we ought to be able to manage, with a little reflection and intelligence. And those are just your great qualities. How does the business strike you?"

Ganimard did not move a muscle. He was willing to stand Lupin's chaff, but his dignity commanded him not to speak a single word in answer nor even to give a nod or shake of the head that might have been taken to express approval or or criticism.

"I see that we are entirely of one mind," continued Lupin, without appearing to remark the chief-inspector's silence. "And I can sum up the matter briefly, as told us by these exhibits. Yesterday evening, between nine and twelve o'clock, a showily dressed young woman was wounded with a knife and then caught round the throat and choked to death by a well-dressed gentleman, wearing a single eyeglass and interested in racing, with whom the aforesaid showily dressed young lady had been eating three meringues and a coffee éclair."

Lupin lit a cigarette and, taking Ganimard by the sleeve:

"Aha, that's up against you, chief-inspector! You thought that, in the domain of police deductions, such feats as those were prohibited to outsiders! Wrong, sir! Lupin juggles with inferences and deductions for all the world like a detective in a novel. My proofs are dazzling and absolutely simple."

And, pointing to the objects one by one, as he demonstrated his statement, he resumed:

"I said, after nine o'clock yesterday evening. This scrap of newspaper bears yesterday's date, with the words, 'Evening edition.' Also, you will see here, pasted to the paper, a bit of one of those yellow wrappers in which the subscribers' copies are sent out. These copies are always delivered by the nine o'clock post. Therefore, it was after nine o'clock. I said, a well-dressed man. Please observe that this tiny piece of glass has the round hole of a single eyeglass at one of the edges and that the single eyeglass is an essentially aristocratic article of wear. This well-dressed man walked into a pastry-cook's shop. Here is the very thin cardboard, shaped like a box, and still showing a little of the cream of the meringues and éclairs box. He also puts in certain things that would have betrayed him, such as the knife, which must have slipped into the Seine. He wraps everything in the newspaper, ties it with the cord and fastens this cut-glass inkstand to it, as a makeweight. Then he makes himself scarce. A little later, the parcel falls into the waterman's barge. And there you are. Oof, it's hot work!... What do you say to the story?"

He looked at Ganimard to see what impression his speech had produced on the inspector. Ganimard did not depart from his attitude of silence.

Lupin began to laugh:

"As a matter of fact, you're annoyed and surprised. But you're suspicious as well: 'Why should that confounded Lupin hand the business over to me,' say you, 'instead of keeping it for himself, hunting down the murderer and rifling his pockets, if there was a robbery?' The question is quite logical, of course. But—there is a 'but'—I have no time, you see. I am full up with work at the present moment: a burglary in London, another at

Lausanne, an exchange of children at Marseilles, to say nothing of having to save a young girl who is at this moment shadowed by death. That's always the way: it never rains but it pours. So I said to myself, 'Suppose I handed the business over to my dear old Ganimard? Now that it is half-solved for him, he is quite capable of succeeding. And what a service I shall be doing him! How magnificently he will be able to distinguish himself!' No sooner said than done. At eight o'clock in the morning, I sent the joker with the orange-peel to meet you. You swallowed the bait; and you were here by nine, all on edge and eager for the fray."

Lupin rose from his chair. He went over to the inspector and, with his eyes in Ganimard's, said:

"That's all. You now know the whole story. Presently, you will know the victim: some ballet-dancer, probably, some singer at a music-hall. On the other hand, the chances are that the criminal lives near the Pont-Neuf, most likely on the left bank. Lastly, here are all the exhibits. I make you a present of them. Set to work. I shall only keep this end of the scarf. If ever you want to piece the scarf together, bring me the other end, the one which the police will find round the victim's neck. Bring it me in four weeks from now to the day, that is to say, on the 29th of December, at ten o'clock in the morning. You can be sure of finding me here. And don't be afraid: this is all perfectly serious, friend of my youth; I swear it is. No humbug, honour bright. You can go straight ahead. Oh, by the way, when you arrest the fellow with the eyeglass, be a bit careful: he is left-handed! Goodbye, old dear, and good luck to you!"

Lupin spun round on his heel, went to the door, opened it and disappeared before Ganimard had even thought of taking a decision. The inspector rushed after him, but at once found that the handle of the door, by some trick of mechanism which he did not know, refused to turn. It took him ten minutes to unscrew the lock and ten minutes more to unscrew the lock of the hall-door. By the time that he had scrambled down the three flights of stairs, Ganimard had given up all hope of catching Arsène Lupin.

Besides, he was not thinking of it. Lupin inspired him with a queer, complex feeling, made up of fear, hatred, involuntary admiration and also the vague instinct that he, Ganimard, in spite of all his efforts, in spite of the persistency of his endeavours, would never get the better of this particular adversary. He pursued him from a sense of duty and pride, but with the continual dread of being taken in by that formidable hoaxer and scouted and fooled in the face of a public that was always only too willing to laugh at the chief-inspector's mishaps.

This business of the red scarf, in particular, struck him as most suspicious. It was interesting, certainly, in more ways than one, but so very improbable! And Lupin's explanation, apparently so logical, would never stand the test of a severe examination!

"No," said Ganimard, "this is all swank: a parcel of suppositions and guesswork based upon nothing at all. I'm not to be caught with chaff."

When he reached the headquarters of police, at 36 Quai des Orfèvres, he had quite made up his mind to treat the incident as though it had never happened.

He went up to the Criminal Investigation Department. Here, one of his fellow-inspectors said:

"Seen the chief?"

"No."

"He was asking for you just now."

"Oh, was he?"

"Yes, you had better go after him."

"Where?"

"To the Rue de Berne... there was a murder there last night."

"Oh! Who's the victim?"

"I don't know exactly... a music-hall singer, I believe."

Ganimard simply muttered:

"By Jove!"

Twenty minutes later he stepped out of the underground railway-station and made for the Rue de Berne.

The victim, who was known in the theatrical world by her stage-name of Jenny Saphir, occupied a small flat on the second floor of one of the houses. A policeman took the chief-inspector upstairs and showed him the way, through two sitting-rooms, to a bedroom, where he found the magistrates in charge of the inquiry, together with the divisional surgeon and M. Dudouis, the head of the detective-service.

Ganimard started at the first glance which he gave into the room. He saw, lying on a sofa, the corpse of a young woman whose hands clutched a strip of red silk! One of the shoulders, which appeared above the low-cut bodice, bore the marks of two wounds surrounded with clotted blood. The distorted and almost blackened features still bore an expression of frenzied terror.

The divisional surgeon, who had just finished his examination, said:

"My first conclusions are very clear. The victim was twice stabbed with a dagger and afterward strangled. The immediate cause of death was asphyxia."

"By Jove!" thought Ganimard again, remembering Lupin's words and the picture which he had drawn of the crime.

The examining-magistrate objected:

"But the neck shows no discoloration."

"She may have been strangled with a napkin or a handkerchief," said the doctor.

"Most probably," said the chief detective, "with this silk scarf, which the victim was wearing and a piece of which remains, as though she had clung to it with her two hands to protect herself."

"But why does only that piece remain?" asked the magistrate. "What has become of the other?"

"The other may have been stained with blood and carried off by the murderer. You can plainly distinguish the hurried slashing of the scissors."

"By Jove!" said Ganimard, between his teeth, for the third time. "That brute of a Lupin saw everything without seeing a thing!"

"And what about the motive of the murder?" asked the magistrate. "The locks have been forced, the cupboards turned upside down. Have you anything to tell me, M. Dudouis?"

The chief of the detective-service replied:

"I can at least suggest a supposition, derived from the statements made by the servant. The victim, who enjoyed a greater reputation on account of her looks than through her talent as a singer, went to Russia, two years ago, and brought back with her a magnificent sapphire, which she appears to have received from some person of importance at the court. Since then, she went by the name of Jenny Saphir and seems generally to have been very proud of that present, although, for prudence sake, she never wore it. I daresay that we shall not be far out if we presume the theft of the sapphire to have been the cause of the crime."

"But did the maid know where the stone was?"

"No, nobody did. And the disorder of the room would tend to prove that the murderer did not know either."

"We will question the maid," said the examining-magistrate.

M. Dudouis took the chief-inspector aside and said:

"You're looking very old-fashioned, Ganimard. What's the matter? Do you suspect anything?"

"Nothing at all, chief."

"That's a pity. We could do with a bit of showy work in the department. This is one of a number of crimes, all of the same class, of which we have failed to discover the perpetrator. This time we want the criminal... and quickly!"

"A difficult job, chief."

"It's got to be done. Listen to me, Ganimard. According to what the maid says, Jenny Saphir led a very regular life. For a month past she was in the habit of frequently receiving visits, on her return from the music-hall, that is to say, at about half-past ten, from a man who would stay until midnight or so. 'He's a society man,' Jenny Saphir used to say, 'and he wants to marry me.' This society man took every precaution to avoid being seen, such as turning up his coat-collar and lowering the brim of his hat when he passed the porter's box. And Jenny Saphir always made a point of sending away her maid, even before he came. This is the man whom we have to find."

"Has he left no traces?"

"None at all. It is obvious that we have to deal with a very clever scoundrel, who prepared his crime beforehand and committed it with every possible chance of escaping unpunished. His arrest would be a great feather in our cap. I rely on you, Ganimard."

"Ah, you rely on me, chief?" replied the inspector. "Well, we shall see... we shall see.... I don't say no.... Only...."

He seemed in a very nervous condition, and his agitation struck M. Dudouis.

"Only," continued Ganimard, "only I swear... do you hear, chief? I swear...."

"What do you swear?"

"Nothing.... We shall see, chief... we shall see...."

Ganimard did not finish his sentence until he was outside, alone. And he finished it aloud, stamping his foot, in a tone of the most violent anger:

"Only, I swear to Heaven that the arrest shall be effected by my own means, without my employing a single one of the clues with which that villain has supplied me. Ah, no! Ah, no!..."

Railing against Lupin, furious at being mixed up in this business and resolved, nevertheless, to get to the bottom of it, he wandered aimlessly about the streets. His brain was seething with irritation; and he tried to adjust his ideas a little and to discover, among the chaotic facts, some trifling detail, unperceived by all, unsuspected by Lupin himself, that might lead him to success.

He lunched hurriedly at a bar, resumed his stroll and suddenly stopped, petrified, astounded and confused. He was walking under the gateway of the very house in the Rue de Surène to which Lupin had enticed him a few hours earlier! A force stronger than his own will was drawing him there once more. The solution of the problem lay there. There and there alone were all the elements of the truth. Do and say what he would, Lupin's assertions were so precise, his calculations so accurate, that, worried to the innermost recesses of his being by so prodigious a display of perspicacity, he could not do other than take up the work at the point where his enemy had left it.

Abandoning all further resistance, he climbed the three flights of stairs. The door of the flat was open. No one had touched the exhibits. He put them in his pocket and walked away.

From that moment, he reasoned and acted, so to speak, mechanically, under the influence of the master whom he could not choose but obey.

Admitting that the unknown person whom he was seeking lived in the neighbourhood of the Pont-Neuf, it became necessary to discover, somewhere between that bridge and the Rue de Berne, the first-class confectioner's shop, open in the evenings, at which the cakes were bought. This did not take long to find. A pastry-cook near the Gare Saint-Lazare showed him some little cardboard boxes, identical in material and shape with the one in Ganimard's possession. Moreover, one of the shop-girls remembered having served, on the previous evening, a gentleman whose face was almost concealed in the collar of his fur coat, but whose eyeglass she had happened to notice.

"That's one clue checked," thought the inspector. "Our man wears an eyeglass."

He next collected the pieces of the racing-paper and showed them to a newsvendor, who easily recognized the *Turf Illustré*. Ganimard at once went to the offices of the *Turf* and asked to see the list of subscribers. Going through the list, he jotted down the names and addresses of all those who lived anywhere near the Pont-Neuf and principally—because Lupin had said so—those on the left bank of the river.

He then went back to the Criminal Investigation Department, took half a dozen men and packed them off with the necessary instructions.

At seven o'clock in the evening, the last of these men returned and brought good news with him. A certain M. Prévailles, a subscriber to the *Turf*, occupied an entresol flat on the Quai des Augustins. On the previous evening, he left his place, wearing a fur coat, took his letters and his paper, the *Turf Illustré*, from the porter's wife, walked away and returned home at midnight. This M. Prévailles wore a single eyeglass. He was a regular race-goer and himself owned several hacks which he either rode himself or jobbed out.

The inquiry had taken so short a time and the results obtained were so exactly in accordance with Lupin's predictions that Ganimard felt quite overcome on hearing the detective's report. Once more he was measuring the prodigious extent of the resources at Lupin's disposal. Never in the course of his life—and Ganimard was already well-advanced in years—had he come across such perspicacity, such a quick and farseeing mind.

He went in search of M. Dudouis.

"Everything's ready, chief. Have you a warrant?"

"Eh?"

"I said, everything is ready for the arrest, chief."

"You know the name of Jenny Saphir's murderer?"

"Yes."

"But how? Explain yourself."

Ganimard had a sort of scruple of conscience, blushed a little and nevertheless replied:

"An accident, chief. The murderer threw everything that was likely to compromise him into the Seine. Part of the parcel was picked up and handed to me."

"By whom?"

"A boatman who refused to give his name, for fear of getting into trouble. But I had all the clues I wanted. It was not so difficult as I expected."

And the inspector described how he had gone to work.

"And you call that an accident!" cried M. Dudouis. "And you say that it was not difficult! Why, it's one of your finest performances! Finish it yourself, Ganimard, and be prudent."

Ganimard was eager to get the business done. He went to the Quai des Augustins with his men and distributed them around the house. He questioned the portress, who said that her tenant took his meals out of doors, but made a point of looking in after dinner.

A little before nine o'clock, in fact, leaning out of her window, she warned Ganimard, who at once gave a low whistle. A gentleman in a tall hat and a fur coat was coming along the pavement beside the Seine. He crossed the road and walked up to the house.

Ganimard stepped forward:

"M. Prévailles, I believe?"

"Yes, but who are you?"

"I have a commission to...."

He had not time to finish his sentence. At the sight of the men appearing out of the shadow, Prévailles quickly retreated to the wall and faced his adversaries, with his back to the door of a shop on the ground-floor, the shutters of which were closed.

"Stand back!" he cried. "I don't know you!"

His right hand brandished a heavy stick, while his left was slipped behind him and seemed to be trying to open the door.

Ganimard had an impression that the man might escape through this way and through some secret outlet:

"None of this nonsense," he said, moving closer to him. "You're caught.... You had better come quietly."

But, just as he was laying hold of Prévailles' stick, Ganimard remembered the warning which Lupin gave him: Prévailles was left-handed; and it was his revolver for which he was feeling behind his back.

The inspector ducked his head. He had noticed the man's sudden movement. Two reports rang out. No one was hit.

A second later, Prévailles received a blow under the chin from the butt-end of a revolver, which brought him down where he stood. He was entered at the Dépôt soon after nine o'clock.

Ganimard enjoyed a great reputation even at that time. But this capture, so quickly effected, by such very simple means, and at once made public by the police, won him a sudden celebrity. Prévailles was forthwith saddled with all the murders that had remained unpunished; and the newspapers vied with one another in extolling Ganimard's prowess.

The case was conducted briskly at the start. It was first of all ascertained that Prévailles, whose real name was Thomas Derocq, had already been in trouble. Moreover, the search instituted in his rooms, while not supplying any fresh proofs, at least led to the discovery of a ball of whipcord similar to the cord used for doing up the parcel and also to the discovery of daggers which would have produced a wound similar to the wounds on the victim.

But, on the eighth day, everything was changed. Until then Prévailles had refused to reply to the questions put to him; but now, assisted by his counsel, he pleaded a circumstantial alibi and maintained that he was at the Folies-Bergère on the night of the murder.

As a matter of fact, the pockets of his dinner-jacket contained the counterfoil of a stall-ticket and a programme of the performance, both bearing the date of that evening.

"An alibi prepared in advance," objected the examining-magistrate.

"Prove it," said Prévailles.

The prisoner was confronted with the witnesses for the prosecution. The young lady from the confectioner's "thought she knew" the gentleman with the eyeglass. The hall-porter in the Rue de Berne "thought he knew" the gentleman who used to come to see Jenny Saphir. But nobody dared to make a more definite statement.

The examination, therefore, led to nothing of a precise character, provided no solid basis whereon to found a serious accusation.

The judge sent for Ganimard and told him of his difficulty.

"I can't possibly persist, at this rate. There is no evidence to support the charge."

"But surely you are convinced in your own mind, *monsieur le juge d'instruction*! Prévailles would never have resisted his arrest unless he was guilty."

"He says that he thought he was being assaulted. He also says that he never set eyes on Jenny Saphir; and, as a matter of fact, we can find no one to contradict his assertion. Then again, admitting that the sapphire has been stolen, we have not been able to find it at his flat."

"Nor anywhere else," suggested Ganimard.

"Quite true, but that is no evidence against him. I'll tell you what we shall want, M. Ganimard, and that very soon: the other end of this red scarf."

"The other end?"

"Yes, for it is obvious that, if the murderer took it away with him, the reason was that the stuff is stained with the marks of the blood on his fingers."

Ganimard made no reply. For several days he had felt that the whole business was tending to this conclusion. There was no other proof possible. Given the silk scarf—and in no other circumstances—Prévailles' guilt was certain. Now Ganimard's position required that Prévailles' guilt should be established. He was responsible for the arrest, it had cast a glamour around him, he had been praised to the skies as the most formidable adversary of criminals; and he would look absolutely ridiculous if Prévailles were released.

Unfortunately, the one and only indispensable proof was in Lupin's pocket. How was he to get hold of it?

Ganimard cast about, exhausted himself with fresh investigations, went over the inquiry from start to finish, spent sleepless nights in turning over the mystery of the Rue de Berne, studied the records of Prévailles' life, sent ten men hunting after the invisible sapphire. Everything was useless.

On the 28th of December, the examining-magistrate stopped him in one of the passages of the Law Courts:

"Well, M. Ganimard, any news?"

"No, *monsieur le juge d'instruction.*"

"Then I shall dismiss the case."

"Wait one day longer."

"What's the use? We want the other end of the scarf; have you got it?"

"I shall have it tomorrow."

"Tomorrow!"

"Yes, but please lend me the piece in your possession."

"What if I do?"

"If you do, I promise to let you have the whole scarf complete."

"Very well, that's understood."

Ganimard followed the examining-magistrate to his room and came out with the piece of silk:

"Hang it all!" he growled. "Yes, I will go and fetch the proof and I shall have it too... always presuming that Master Lupin has the courage to keep the appointment."

In point of fact, he did not doubt for a moment that Master Lupin would have this courage, and that was just what exasperated him. Why had Lupin insisted on this meeting? What was his object, in the circumstances?

Anxious, furious and full of hatred, he resolved to take every precaution necessary not only to prevent his falling into a trap himself, but to make his enemy fall into one, now that the opportunity offered. And, on the next day, which was the 29th of December, the date fixed by Lupin, after spending the night in studying the old manor-house in the Rue de Surène and convincing himself that there was no other outlet than the front door, he warned his men that he was going on a dangerous expedition and arrived with them on the field of battle.

He posted them in a café and gave them formal instructions: if he showed himself at one of the third-floor windows, or if he failed to return within an hour, the detectives were to enter the house and arrest anyone who tried to leave it.

The chief-inspector made sure that his revolver was in working order and that he could take it from his pocket easily. Then he went upstairs.

He was surprised to find things as he had left them, the doors open and the locks broken. After ascertaining that the windows of the principal room looked out on the street, he visited the three other rooms that made up the flat. There was no one there.

"Master Lupin was afraid," he muttered, not without a certain satisfaction.

"Don't be silly," said a voice behind him.

Turning round, he saw an old workman, wearing a house-painter's long smock, standing in the doorway.

"You needn't bother your head," said the man. "It's I, Lupin. I have been working in the painter's shop since early morning. This is when we knock off for breakfast. So I came upstairs."

He looked at Ganimard with a quizzing smile and cried:

"'Pon my word, this is a gorgeous moment I owe you, old chap! I wouldn't sell it for ten years of your life; and yet you know how I love you! What do you think of it, artist? Wasn't it well thought out and well foreseen? Foreseen from alpha to omega? Did I understand the business? Did I penetrate the mystery of the scarf? I'm not saying that there were no holes in my argument, no links missing in the chain.... But what a masterpiece of intelligence! Ganimard, what a reconstruction of events! What an intuition of everything that had taken place and of everything that was going to take place, from the discovery of the crime to your arrival here in search of a proof! What really marvellous divination! Have you the scarf?"

"Yes, half of it. Have you the other?"

"Here it is. Let's compare."

They spread the two pieces of silk on the table. The cuts made by the scissors corresponded exactly. Moreover, the colours were identical.

"But I presume," said Lupin, "that this was not the only thing you came for. What you are interested in seeing is the marks of the blood. Come with me, Ganimard: it's rather dark in here."

They moved into the next room, which, though it overlooked the courtyard, was lighter; and Lupin held his piece of silk against the windowpane:

"Look," he said, making room for Ganimard.

The inspector gave a start of delight. The marks of the five fingers and the print of the palm were distinctly visible. The evidence was undeniable. The murderer had seized the stuff in his bloodstained hand, in the same hand that had stabbed Jenny Saphir, and tied the scarf round her neck.

"And it is the print of a left hand," observed Lupin. "Hence my warning, which had nothing miraculous about it, you see. For, though I admit, friend of my youth, that you may look upon me as a superior intelligence, I won't have you treat me as a wizard."

Ganimard had quickly pocketed the piece of silk. Lupin nodded his head in approval:

"Quite right, old boy, it's for you. I'm so glad you're glad! And, you see, there was no trap about all this... only the wish to oblige... a service between friends, between pals.... And also, I confess, a little curiosity.... Yes, I wanted to examine this other piece of silk, the one the police had.... Don't be afraid: I'll give it back to you.... Just a second...."

Lupin, with a careless movement, played with the tassel at the end of this half of the scarf, while Ganimard listened to him in spite of himself:

68

"How ingenious these little bits of women's work are! Did you notice one detail in the maid's evidence? Jenny Saphir was very handy with her needle and used to make all her own hats and frocks. It is obvious that she made this scarf herself.... Besides, I noticed that from the first. I am naturally curious, as I have already told you, and I made a thorough examination of the piece of silk which you have just put in your pocket. Inside the tassel, I found a little sacred medal, which the poor girl had stitched into it to bring her luck. Touching, isn't it, Ganimard? A little medal of Our Lady of Good Succour."

The inspector felt greatly puzzled and did not take his eyes off the other. And Lupin continued:

"Then I said to myself, 'How interesting it would be to explore the other half of the scarf, the one which the police will find round the victim's neck!' For this other half, which I hold in my hands at last, is finished off in the same way... so I shall be able to see if it has a hiding-place too and what's inside it.... But look, my friend, isn't it cleverly made? And so simple! All you have to do is to take a skein of red cord and braid it round a wooden cup, leaving a little recess, a little empty space in the middle, very small, of course, but large enough to hold a medal of a saint... or anything.... A precious stone, for instance.... Such as a sapphire...."

At that moment he finished pushing back the silk cord and, from the hollow of a cup he took between his thumb and forefinger a wonderful blue stone, perfect in respect of size and purity.

"Ha! What did I tell you, friend of my youth?"

He raised his head. The inspector had turned livid and was staring wild-eyed, as though fascinated by the stone that sparkled before him. He at last realized the whole plot:

"You dirty scoundrel!" he muttered, repeating the insults which he had used at the first interview. "You scum of the earth!"

The two men were standing one against the other.

"Give me back that," said the inspector.

Lupin held out the piece of silk.

"And the sapphire," said Ganimard, in a peremptory tone.

"Don't be silly."

"Give it back, or...."

"Or what, you idiot!" cried Lupin. "Look here, do you think I put you on to this soft thing for nothing?"

"Give it back!"

"You haven't noticed what I've been about, that's plain! What! For four weeks I've kept you on the move like a deer; and you want to...! Come, Ganimard, old chap, pull yourself together!... Don't you see that you've been playing the good dog for four weeks on end?... Fetch it, Rover!... There's a nice blue pebble over there, which master can't get at. Hunt it, Ganimard, fetch it... bring it to master.... Ah, he's his master's own good little dog!... Sit up! Beg!... Does'ms want a bit of sugar, then?..."

Ganimard, containing the anger that seethed within him, thought only of one thing, summoning his detectives. And, as the room in which he now was looked out on the courtyard, he tried gradually to work his way round to the communicating door. He would then run to the window and break one of the panes.

"All the same," continued Lupin, "what a pack of dunderheads you and the rest must be! You've had the silk all this time and not one of you ever thought of feeling it, not one of you ever asked himself the reason why the poor girl hung on to her scarf. Not one of you! You just acted at haphazard, without reflecting, without foreseeing anything...."

The inspector had attained his object. Taking advantage of a second when Lupin had turned away from him, he suddenly wheeled round and grasped the door-handle. But an oath escaped him: the handle did not budge.

Lupin burst into a fit of laughing:

"Not even that! You did not even foresee that! You lay a trap for me and you won't admit that I may perhaps smell the thing out beforehand.... And you allow yourself to be brought into this room without asking whether I am not bringing you here for a particular reason and without remembering that the locks are fitted with a special mechanism. Come now, speaking frankly, what do you think of it yourself?"

"What do I think of it?" roared Ganimard, beside himself with rage.

He had drawn his revolver and was pointing it straight at Lupin's face.

"Hands up!" he cried. "That's what I think of it!"

Lupin placed himself in front of him and shrugged his shoulders:

"Sold again!" he said.

"Hands up, I say, once more!"

"And sold again, say I. Your deadly weapon won't go off."

"What?"

"Old Catherine, your housekeeper, is in my service. She damped the charges this morning while you were having your breakfast coffee."

Ganimard made a furious gesture, pocketed the revolver and rushed at Lupin.

"Well?" said Lupin, stopping him short with a well-aimed kick on the shin.

Their clothes were almost touching. They exchanged defiant glances, the glances of two adversaries who mean to come to blows. Nevertheless, there was no fight. The recollection of the earlier struggles made any present struggle useless. And Ganimard, who remembered all his past failures, his vain attacks, Lupin's crushing reprisals, did not lift a limb. There was nothing to be done. He felt it. Lupin had forces at his command against which any individual force simply broke to pieces. So what was the good?

"I agree," said Lupin, in a friendly voice, as though answering Ganimard's unspoken thought, "you would do better to let things be as they are. Besides, friend of my youth, think of all that this incident has brought you: fame, the certainty of quick promotion and, thanks to that, the prospect of a happy and comfortable old age! Surely, you don't want the discovery of the sapphire and the head of poor Arsène Lupin in addition! It wouldn't be fair. To say nothing of the fact that poor Arsène Lupin saved your life.... Yes, sir! Who warned you, at this very spot, that Prévailles was left-handed?... And is this the way you thank me? It's not pretty of you, Ganimard. Upon my word, you make me blush for you!"

While chattering, Lupin had gone through the same performance as Ganimard and was now near the door. Ganimard saw that his foe was about to escape him. Forgetting all prudence, he tried to block his way and received a tremendous butt in the stomach, which sent him rolling to the opposite wall.

Lupin dexterously touched a spring, turned the handle, opened the door and slipped away, roaring with laughter as he went.

Twenty minutes later, when Ganimard at last succeeded in joining his men, one of them said to him:

"A house-painter left the house, as his mates were coming back from breakfast, and put a letter in my hand. 'Give that to your governor,' he said. 'Which governor?' I asked; but he was gone. I suppose it's meant for you."

"Let's have it."

Ganimard opened the letter. It was hurriedly scribbled in pencil and contained these words:

"This is to warn you, friend of my youth, against excessive credulity. When a fellow tells you that the cartridges in your revolver are damp, however great your confidence in that fellow may be, even though his name be Arsène Lupin, never allow yourself to be taken in. Fire first; and, if the fellow hops the twig, you will have acquired the proof (1) that the cartridges are not damp; and (2) that old Catherine is the most honest and respectable of housekeepers.

"One of these days, I hope to have the pleasure of making her acquaintance.

"Meanwhile, friend of my youth, believe me always affectionately and sincerely yours,

"ARSÈNE LUPIN."

VI

SHADOWED BY DEATH

After he had been round the walls of the property, Arsène Lupin returned to the spot from which he started. It was perfectly clear to him that there was no breach in the walls; and the only way of entering the extensive grounds of the Château de Maupertuis was through a little low door, firmly bolted on the inside, or through the principal gate, which was overlooked by the lodge.

"Very well," he said. "We must employ heroic methods."

Pushing his way into the copsewood where he had hidden his motor-bicycle, he unwound a length of twine from under the saddle and went to a place which he had noticed in the course of his exploration. At this place, which was situated far from the road, on the edge of a wood, a number of large trees, standing inside the park, overlapped the wall.

Lupin fastened a stone to the end of the string, threw it up and caught a thick branch, which he drew down to him and bestraddled. The branch, in recovering its position, raised him from the ground. He climbed over the wall, slipped down the tree, and sprang lightly on the grass.

It was winter; and, through the leafless boughs, across the undulating lawns, he could see the little Château de Maupertuis in the distance. Fearing lest he should be perceived, he concealed himself behind a clump of fir-trees. From there, with the aid of a field-glass, he studied the dark and melancholy front of the manor-house. All the windows were closed and, as it were, barricaded with solid shutters. The house might easily have been uninhabited.

"By Jove!" muttered Lupin. "It's not the liveliest of residences. I shall certainly not come here to end my days!"

But the clock struck three; one of the doors on the ground-floor opened; and the figure of a woman appeared, a very slender figure wrapped in a brown cloak.

The woman walked up and down for a few minutes and was at once surrounded by birds, to which she scattered crumbs of bread. Then she went down the stone steps that led to the middle lawn and skirted it, taking the path on the right.

With his field-glass, Lupin could distinctly see her coming in his direction. She was tall, fair-haired, graceful in appearance, and seemed to be quite a young girl. She walked with a sprightly step, looking at the pale December sun and amusing herself by breaking the little dead twigs on the shrubs along the road.

She had gone nearly two thirds of the distance that separated her from Lupin when there came a furious sound of barking and a huge dog, a colossal Danish boarhound, sprang from a neighbouring kennel and stood erect at the end of the chain by which it was fastened.

The girl moved a little to one side, without paying further attention to what was doubtless a daily incident. The dog grew angrier than ever, standing on its legs and dragging at its collar, at the risk of strangling itself.

Thirty or forty steps farther, yielding probably to an impulse of impatience, the girl turned round and made a gesture with her hand. The great Dane gave a start of rage, retreated to the back of its kennel and rushed out again, this time unfettered. The girl uttered a cry of mad terror. The dog was covering the space between them, trailing its broken chain behind it.

She began to run, to run with all her might, and screamed out desperately for help. But the dog came up with her in a few bounds.

She fell, at once exhausted, giving herself up for lost. The animal was already upon her, almost touching her.

At that exact moment a shot rang out. The dog turned a complete somersault, recovered its feet, tore the ground and then lay down, giving a number of hoarse, breathless howls, which ended in a dull moan and an indistinct gurgling. And that was all.

"Dead," said Lupin, who had hastened up at once, prepared, if necessary, to fire his revolver a second time.

The girl had risen and stood pale, still staggering. She looked in great surprise at this man whom she did not know and who had saved her life; and she whispered:

"Thank you.... I have had a great fright.... You were in the nick of time.... I thank you, monsieur."

Lupin took off his hat:

"Allow me to introduce myself, mademoiselle.... My name is Paul Daubreuil.... But before entering into any explanations, I must ask for one moment...."

He stooped over the dog's dead body and examined the chain at the part where the brute's effort had snapped it:

"That's it," he said, between his teeth. "It's just as I suspected. By Jupiter, things are moving rapidly!... I ought to have come earlier."

Returning to the girl's side, he said to her, speaking very quickly:

"Mademoiselle, we have not a minute to lose. My presence in these grounds is quite irregular. I do not wish to be surprised here; and this for reasons that concern yourself alone. Do you think that the report can have been heard at the house?"

The girl seemed already to have recovered from her emotion; and she replied, with a calmness that revealed all her pluck:

"I don't think so."

"Is your father in the house today?"

"My father is ill and has been in bed for months. Besides, his room looks out on the other front."

"And the servants?"

"Their quarters and the kitchen are also on the other side. No one ever comes to this part. I walk here myself, but nobody else does."

"It is probable, therefore, that I have not been seen either, especially as the trees hide us?"

"It is most probable."

"Then I can speak to you freely?"

73

"Certainly, but I don't understand...."

"You will, presently. Permit me to be brief. The point is this: four days ago, Mlle. Jeanne Darcieux...."

"That is my name," she said, smiling.

"Mlle. Jeanne Darcieux," continued Lupin, "wrote a letter to one of her friends, called Marceline, who lives at Versailles...."

"How do you know all that?" asked the girl, in astonishment. "I tore up the letter before I had finished it."

"And you flung the pieces on the edge of the road that runs from the house to Vendôme."

"That's true.... I had gone out walking...."

"The pieces were picked up and they came into my hands next day."

"Then... you must have read them," said Jeanne Darcieux, betraying a certain annoyance by her manner.

"Yes, I committed that indiscretion; and I do not regret it, because I can save you."

"Save me? From what?"

"From death."

Lupin spoke this little sentence in a very distinct voice. The girl gave a shudder. Then she said:

"I am not threatened with death."

"Yes, you are, mademoiselle. At the end of October, you were reading on a bench on the terrace where you were accustomed to sit at the same hour every day, when a block of stone fell from the cornice above your head and you were within a few inches of being crushed."

"An accident...."

"One fine evening in November, you were walking in the kitchen-garden, by moonlight. A shot was fired. The bullet whizzed past your ear."

"At least, I thought so."

"Lastly, less than a week ago, the little wooden bridge that crosses the river in the park, two yards from the waterfall, gave way while you were on it. You were just able, by a miracle, to catch hold of the root of a tree."

Jeanne Darcieux tried to smile.

"Very well. But, as I wrote to Marceline, these are only a series of coincidences, of accidents...."

"No, mademoiselle, no. One accident of this sort is allowable.... So are two... and even then!... But we have no right to suppose that the chapter of accidents, repeating the same act three times in such different and extraordinary circumstances, is a mere amusing coincidence. That is why I thought that I might presume to come to your assistance. And, as my intervention can be of no use unless it remains secret, I did not hesitate to make my way in here... without walking through the gate. I came in the nick of time, as you said. Your enemy was attacking you once more."

"What!... Do you think?... No, it is impossible.... I refuse to believe...."

Lupin picked up the chain and, showing it to her:

"Look at the last link. There is no question but that it has been filed. Otherwise, so powerful a chain as this would never have yielded. Besides, you can see the mark of the file here."

Jeanne turned pale and her pretty features were distorted with terror:

"But who can bear me such a grudge?" she gasped. "It is terrible.... I have never done anyone harm.... And yet you are certainly right.... Worse still...."

She finished her sentence in a lower voice:

"Worse still, I am wondering whether the same danger does not threaten my father."

"Has he been attacked also?"

"No, for he never stirs from his room. But his is such a mysterious illness!... He has no strength... he cannot walk at all.... In addition to that, he is subject to fits of suffocation, as though his heart stopped beating.... Oh, what an awful thing!"

Lupin realized all the authority which he was able to assert at such a moment, and he said:

"Have no fear, mademoiselle. If you obey me blindly, I shall be sure to succeed."

"Yes... yes... I am quite willing... but all this is so terrible...."

"Trust me, I beg of you. And please listen to me, I shall want a few particulars."

He rapped out a number of questions, which Jeanne Darcieux answered hurriedly:

"That animal was never let loose, was he?"

"Never."

"Who used to feed him?"

"The lodge-keeper. He brought him his food every evening."

"Consequently, he could go near him without being bitten?"

"Yes; and he only, for the dog was very savage."

"You don't suspect the man?"

"Oh, no!... Baptiste?... Never!"

"And you can't think of anybody?"

"No. Our servants are quite devoted to us. They are very fond of me."

"You have no friends staying in the house?"

"No."

"No brother?"

"No."

"Then your father is your only protector?"

"Yes; and I have told you the condition he is in."

"Have you told him of the different attempts?"

"Yes; and it was wrong of me to do so. Our doctor, old Dr. Guéroult, forbade me to cause him the least excitement."

"Your mother?..."

"I don't remember her. She died sixteen years ago... just sixteen years ago."

"How old were you then?"

"I was not quite five years old."

"And were you living here?"

"We were living in Paris. My father only bought this place the year after."

Lupin was silent for a few moments. Then he concluded:

"Very well, mademoiselle, I am obliged to you. Those particulars are all I need for the present. Besides, it would not be wise for us to remain together longer."

"But," she said, "the lodge-keeper will find the dog soon.... Who will have killed him?"

"You, mademoiselle, to defend yourself against an attack."

"I never carry firearms."

"I am afraid you do," said Lupin, smiling, "because you killed the dog and there is no one but you who could have killed him. For that matter, let them think what they please. The great thing is that I shall not be suspected when I come to the house."

"To the house? Do you intend to?"

"Yes. I don't yet know how... But I shall come.... This very evening.... So, once more, be easy in your mind. I will answer for everything."

Jeanne looked at him and, dominated by him, conquered by his air of assurance and good faith, she said, simply:

"I am quite easy."

"Then all will go well. Till this evening, mademoiselle."

"Till this evening."

She walked away; and Lupin, following her with his eyes until the moment when she disappeared round the corner of the house, murmured:

"What a pretty creature! It would be a pity if any harm were to come to her. Luckily, Arsène Lupin is keeping his weather-eye open."

Taking care not to be seen, with eyes and ears attentive to the least sight or sound, he inspected every nook and corner of the grounds, looked for the little low door which he had noticed outside and which was the door of the kitchen garden, drew the bolt, took the key and then skirted the walls and found himself once more near the tree which he had climbed. Two minutes later, he was mounting his motorcycle.

The village of Maupertuis lay quite close to the estate. Lupin inquired and learnt that Dr. Guéroult lived next door to the church.

He rang, was shown into the consulting-room and introduced himself by his name of Paul Daubreuil, of the Rue de Surène, Paris, adding that he had official relations with the detective-service, a fact which he requested might be kept secret. He had become acquainted, by means of a torn letter, with the incidents that had endangered Mlle. Darcieux's life; and he had come to that young lady's assistance.

Dr. Guéroult, an old country practitioner, who idolized Jeanne, on hearing Lupin's explanations at once admitted that those incidents constituted undeniable proofs of a plot. He showed great concern, offered his visitor hospitality and kept him to dinner.

The two men talked at length. In the evening, they walked round to the manor-house together.

The doctor went to the sick man's room, which was on the first floor, and asked leave to bring up a young colleague, to whom he intended soon to make over his practice, when he retired.

Lupin, on entering, saw Jeanne Darcieux seated by her father's bedside. She suppressed a movement of surprise and, at a sign from the doctor, left the room.

The consultation thereupon took place in Lupin's presence. M. Darcieux's face was worn, with much suffering and his eyes were bright with fever. He complained particularly, that day, of his heart. After the auscultation, he questioned the doctor with obvious anxiety; and each reply seemed to give him relief. He also spoke of Jeanne and expressed his conviction that they were deceiving him and that his daughter had escaped yet more accidents. He continued perturbed, in spite of the doctor's denials. He wanted to have the police informed and inquiries set on foot.

But his excitement tired him and he gradually dropped off to sleep.

Lupin stopped the doctor in the passage:

"Come, doctor, give me your exact opinion. Do you think that M. Darcieux's illness can be attributed to an outside cause?"

"How do you mean?"

"Well, suppose that the same enemy should be interested in removing both father and daughter."

The doctor seemed struck by the suggestion.

"Upon my word, there is something in what you say.... The father's illness at times adopts such a very unusual character!... For instance, the paralysis of the legs, which is almost complete, ought to be accompanied by...."

The doctor reflected for a moment and then said in a low voice:

"You think it's poison, of course... but what poison?... Besides, I see no toxic symptoms.... It would have to be.... But what are you doing? What's the matter?..."

The two men were talking outside a little sitting-room on the first floor, where Jeanne, seizing the opportunity while the doctor was with her father, had begun her evening meal. Lupin, who was watching her through the open door, saw her lift a cup to her lips and take a few sups.

Suddenly, he rushed at her and caught her by the arm:

"What are you drinking there?"

"Why," she said, taken aback, "only tea!"

"You pulled a face of disgust... what made you do that?"

"I don't know... I thought...."

"You thought what?"

"That... that it tasted rather bitter.... But I expect that comes from the medicine I mixed with it."

"What medicine?"

"Some drops which I take at dinner... the drops which you prescribed for me, you know, doctor."

"Yes," said Dr. Guéroult, "but that medicine has no taste of any kind.... You know it hasn't, Jeanne, for you have been taking it for a fortnight and this is the first time...."

"Quite right," said the girl, "and this does have a taste.... There—oh!—my mouth is still burning."

Dr. Guéroult now took a sip from the cup; "Faugh!" he exclaimed, spitting it out again. "There's no mistake about it...."

Lupin, on his side, was examining the bottle containing the medicine; and he asked:

"Where is this bottle kept in the daytime?"

But Jeanne was unable to answer. She had put her hand to her heart and, wan-faced, with staring eyes, seemed to be suffering great pain:

"It hurts... it hurts," she stammered.

The two men quickly carried her to her room and laid her on the bed:

"She ought to have an emetic," said Lupin.

"Open the cupboard," said the doctor. "You'll see a medicine-case.... Have you got it?... Take out one of those little tubes.... Yes, that one.... And now some hot water.... You'll find some on the tea-tray in the other room."

Jeanne's own maid came running up in answer to the bell. Lupin told her that Mlle. Darcieux had been taken unwell, for some unknown reason.

He next returned to the little dining-room, inspected the sideboard and the cupboards, went down to the kitchen and pretended that the doctor had sent him to ask about M. Darcieux's diet. Without appearing to do so, he catechized the cook, the butler, and Baptiste, the lodge-keeper, who had his meals at the manor-house with the servants. Then he went back to the doctor:

"Well?"

"She's asleep."

"Any danger?"

"No. Fortunately, she had only taken two or three sips. But this is the second time today that you have saved her life, as the analysis of this bottle will show."

"Quite superfluous to make an analysis, doctor. There is no doubt about the fact that there has been an attempt at poisoning."

"By whom?"

"I can't say. But the demon who is engineering all this business clearly knows the ways of the house. He comes and goes as he pleases, walks about in the park, files the dog's chain, mixes poison with the food and, in short, moves and acts precisely as though he were living the very life of her—or rather of those—whom he wants to put away."

"Ah! You really believe that M. Darcieux is threatened with the same danger?"

"I have not a doubt of it."

"Then it must be one of the servants? But that is most unlikely! Do you think...?"

"I think nothing, doctor. I know nothing. All I can say is that the situation is most tragic and that we must be prepared for the worst. Death is here, doctor, shadowing the people in this house; and it will soon strike at those whom it is pursuing."

"What's to be done?"

"Watch, doctor. Let us pretend that we are alarmed about M. Darcieux's health and spend the night in here. The bedrooms of both the father and daughter are close by. If anything happens, we are sure to hear."

There was an easy-chair in the room. They arranged to sleep in it turn and turn about.

In reality, Lupin slept for only two or three hours. In the middle of the night he left the room, without disturbing his companion, carefully looked round the whole of the house and walked out through the principal gate.

He reached Paris on his motorcycle at nine o'clock in the morning. Two of his friends, to whom he telephoned on the road, met him there. They all three spent the day in making searches which Lupin had planned out beforehand.

He set out again hurriedly at six o'clock; and never, perhaps, as he told me subsequently, did he risk his life with greater temerity than in his breakneck ride, at a mad rate of speed, on a foggy December evening, with the light of his lamp hardly able to pierce through the darkness.

He sprang from his bicycle outside the gate, which was still open, ran to the house and reached the first floor in a few bounds.

There was no one in the little dining-room.

Without hesitating, without knocking, he walked into Jeanne's bedroom:

"Ah, here you are!" he said, with a sigh of relief, seeing Jeanne and the doctor sitting side by side, talking.

"What? Any news?" asked the doctor, alarmed at seeing such a state of agitation in a man whose coolness he had had occasion to observe.

"No," said Lupin. "No news. And here?"

"None here, either. We have just left M. Darcieux. He has had an excellent day and he ate his dinner with a good appetite. As for Jeanne, you can see for yourself, she has all her pretty colour back again."

"Then she must go."

"Go? But it's out of the question!" protested the girl.

"You must go, you must!" cried Lupin, with real violence, stamping his foot on the floor.

He at once mastered himself, spoke a few words of apology and then, for three or four minutes, preserved a complete silence, which the doctor and Jeanne were careful not to disturb.

At last, he said to the young girl:

"You shall go tomorrow morning, mademoiselle. It will be only for one or two weeks. I will take you to your friend at Versailles, the one to whom you were writing. I entreat you to get everything ready tonight… without concealment of any kind. Let the servants know that you are going…. On the other hand, the doctor will be good enough to tell M. Darcieux and give him to understand, with every possible precaution, that this journey is essential to your safety. Besides, he can join you as soon as his strength permits…. That's settled, is it not?"

"Yes," she said, absolutely dominated by Lupin's gentle and imperious voice.

"In that case," he said, "be as quick as you can… and do not stir from your room…."

"But," said the girl, with a shudder, "am I to stay alone tonight?"

"Fear nothing. Should there be the least danger, the doctor and I will come back. Do not open your door unless you hear three very light taps."

Jeanne at once rang for her maid. The doctor went to M. Darcieux, while Lupin had some supper brought to him in the little dining-room.

"That's done," said the doctor, returning to him in twenty minutes' time. "M. Darcieux did not raise any great difficulty. As a matter of fact, he himself thinks it just as well that we should send Jeanne away."

They then went downstairs together and left the house.

On reaching the lodge, Lupin called the keeper.

"You can shut the gate, my man. If M. Darcieux should want us, send for us at once."

The clock of Maupertuis church struck ten. The sky was overcast with black clouds, through which the moon broke at moments.

The two men walked on for sixty or seventy yards.

They were nearing the village, when Lupin gripped his companion by the arm:

"Stop!"

"What on earth's the matter?" exclaimed the doctor.

"The matter is this," Lupin jerked out, "that, if my calculations turn out right, if I have not misjudged the business from start to finish, Mlle. Darcieux will be murdered before the night is out."

"Eh? What's that?" gasped the doctor, in dismay. "But then why did we go?"

"With the precise object that the miscreant, who is watching all our movements in the dark, may not postpone his crime and may perpetrate it, not at the hour chosen by himself, but at the hour which I have decided upon."

"Then we are returning to the manor-house?"

"Yes, of course we are, but separately."

"In that case, let us go at once."

"Listen to me, doctor," said Lupin, in a steady voice, "and let us waste no time in useless words. Above all, we must defeat any attempt to watch us. You will therefore go straight home and not come out again until you are quite certain that you have not been followed. You will then make for the walls of the property, keeping to the left, till you come to the little door of the kitchen-garden. Here is the key. When the church clock strikes eleven, open the door very gently and walk right up to the terrace at the back of the house. The fifth window is badly fastened. You have only to climb over the balcony. As soon as you are inside Mlle. Darcieux's room, bolt the door and don't budge. You quite understand, don't budge, either of you, whatever happens. I have noticed that Mlle. Darcieux leaves her dressing-room window ajar, isn't that so?"

"Yes, it's a habit which I taught her."

"That's the way they'll come."

"And you?"

"That's the way I shall come also."

"And do you know who the villain is?"

Lupin hesitated and then replied:

"No, I don't know.... And that is just how we shall find out. But, I implore you, keep cool. Not a word, not a movement, *whatever happens*!"

"I promise you."

"I want more than that, doctor. You must give me your word of honour."

"I give you my word of honour."

The doctor went away. Lupin at once climbed a neighbouring mound from which he could see the windows of the first and second floor. Several of them were lighted.

He waited for some little time. The lights went out one by one. Then, taking a direction opposite to that in which the doctor had gone, he branched off to the right and skirted the wall until he came to the clump of trees near which he had hidden his motorcycle on the day before.

80

Eleven o'clock struck. He calculated the time which it would take the doctor to cross the kitchen-garden and make his way into the house.

"That's one point scored!" he muttered. "Everything's all right on that side. And now, Lupin to the rescue? The enemy won't be long before he plays his last trump... and, by all the gods, I must be there!..."

He went through the same performance as on the first occasion, pulled down the branch and hoisted himself to the top of the wall, from which he was able to reach the bigger boughs of the tree.

Just then he pricked up his ears. He seemed to hear a rustling of dead leaves. And he actually perceived a dark form moving on the level thirty yards away:

"Hang it all!" he said to himself. "I'm done: the scoundrel has smelt a rat."

A moonbeam pierced through the clouds. Lupin distinctly saw the man take aim. He tried to jump to the ground and turned his head. But he felt something hit him in the chest, heard the sound of a report, uttered an angry oath and came crashing down from branch to branch, like a corpse.

Meanwhile, Doctor Guéroult, following Arsène Lupin's instructions, had climbed the ledge of the fifth window and groped his way to the first floor. On reaching Jeanne's room, he tapped lightly, three times, at the door and, immediately on entering, pushed the bolt:

"Lie down at once," he whispered to the girl, who had not taken off her things. "You must appear to have gone to bed. *Brrrr*, it's cold in here! Is the window open in your dressing-room?"

"Yes... would you like me to...?"

"No, leave it as it is. They are coming."

"They are coming!" spluttered Jeanne, in affright.

"Yes, beyond a doubt."

"But who? Do you suspect anyone?"

"I don't know who.... I expect that there is someone hidden in the house... or in the park."

"Oh, I feel so frightened!"

"Don't be frightened. The sportsman who's looking after you seems jolly clever and makes a point of playing a safe game. I expect he's on the lookout in the court."

The doctor put out the night-light, went to the window and raised the blind. A narrow cornice, running along the first story, prevented him from seeing more than a distant part of the courtyard; and he came back and sat down by the bed.

Some very painful minutes passed, minutes that appeared to them interminably long. The clock in the village struck; but, taken up as they were with all the little noises of the night, they hardly noticed the sound. They listened, listened, with all their nerves on edge:

"Did you hear?" whispered the doctor.

"Yes... yes," said Jeanne, sitting up in bed.

81

"Lie down... lie down," he said, presently. "There's someone coming."

There was a little tapping sound outside, against the cornice. Next came a series of indistinct noises, the nature of which they could not make out for certain. But they had a feeling that the window in the dressing-room was being opened wider, for they were buffeted by gusts of cold air.

Suddenly, it became quite clear: there was someone next door.

The doctor, whose hand was trembling a little, seized his revolver. Nevertheless, he did not move, remembering the formal orders which he had received and fearing to act against them.

The room was in absolute darkness; and they were unable to see where the adversary was. But they felt his presence.

They followed his invisible movements, the sound of his footsteps deadened by the carpet; and they did not doubt but that he had already crossed the threshold of the room.

And the adversary stopped. Of that they were certain. He was standing six steps away from the bed, motionless, undecided perhaps, seeking to pierce the darkness with his keen eyes.

Jeanne's hand, icy-cold and clammy, trembled in the doctor's grasp.

With his other hand, the doctor clutched his revolver, with his finger on the trigger. In spite of his pledged word, he did not hesitate. If the adversary touched the end of the bed, the shot would be fired at a venture.

The adversary took another step and then stopped again. And there was something awful about that silence, that impassive silence, that darkness in which those human beings were peering at one another, wildly.

Who was it looming in the murky darkness? Who was the man? What horrible enmity was it that turned his hand against the girl and what abominable aim was he pursuing?

Terrified though they were, Jeanne and the doctor thought only of that one thing: to see, to learn the truth, to gaze upon the adversary's face.

He took one more step and did not move again. It seemed to them that his figure stood out, darker, against the dark space and that his arm rose slowly, slowly....

A minute passed and then another minute....

And, suddenly, beyond the man, on the right a sharp click.... A bright light flashed, was flung upon the man, lit him full in the face, remorselessly.

Jeanne gave a cry of affright. She had seen—standing over her, with a dagger in his hand—she had seen... her father!

Almost at the same time, though the light was already turned off, there came a report: the doctor had fired.

"Dash it all, don't shoot!" roared Lupin.

He threw his arms round the doctor, who choked out:

"Didn't you see?... Didn't you see?... Listen!... He's escaping!..."

"Let him escape: it's the best thing that could happen."

He pressed the spring of his electric lantern again, ran to the dressing-room, made certain that the man had disappeared and, returning quietly to the table, lit the lamp.

Jeanne lay on her bed, pallid, in a dead faint.

The doctor, huddled in his chair, emitted inarticulate sounds.

"Come," said Lupin, laughing, "pull yourself together. There is nothing to excite ourselves about: it's all over."

"Her father!... Her father!" moaned the old doctor.

"If you please, doctor, Mlle. Darcieux is ill. Look after her."

Without more words, Lupin went back to the dressing-room and stepped out on the window-ledge. A ladder stood against the ledge. He ran down it. Skirting the wall of the house, twenty steps farther, he tripped over the rungs of a rope-ladder, which he climbed and found himself in M. Darcieux's bedroom. The room was empty.

"Just so," he said. "My gentleman did not like the position and has cleared out. Here's wishing him a good journey.... And, of course, the door is bolted?... Exactly!... That is how our sick man, tricking his worthy medical attendant, used to get up at night in full security, fasten his rope-ladder to the balcony and prepare his little games. He's no fool, is friend Darcieux!"

He drew the bolts and returned to Jeanne's room. The doctor, who was just coming out of the doorway, drew him to the little dining-room:

"She's asleep, don't let us disturb her. She has had a bad shock and will take some time to recover."

Lupin poured himself out a glass of water and drank it down. Then he took a chair and, calmly:

"Pooh! She'll be all right by tomorrow."

"What do you say?"

"I say that she'll be all right by tomorrow."

"Why?"

"In the first place, because it did not strike me that Mlle. Darcieux felt any very great affection for her father."

"Never mind! Think of it: a father who tries to kill his daughter! A father who, for months on end, repeats his monstrous attempt four, five, six times over again!... Well, isn't that enough to blight a less sensitive soul than Jeanne's for good and all? What a hateful memory!"

"She will forget."

"One does not forget such a thing as that."

"She will forget, doctor, and for a very simple reason...."

"Explain yourself!"

"She is not M. Darcieux's daughter!"

"Eh?"

"I repeat, she is not that villain's daughter."

"What do you mean? M. Darcieux...."

"M. Darcieux is only her stepfather. She had just been born when her father, her real father, died. Jeanne's mother then married a cousin of her husband's, a man bearing the same name, and she died within a year of her second wedding. She left Jeanne in M. Darcieux's charge. He first took her abroad and then bought this country-house; and, as nobody knew him in the neighbourhood, he represented the child as being his daughter. She herself did not know the truth about her birth."

The doctor sat confounded. He asked:

"Are you sure of your facts?"

"I spent my day in the town-halls of the Paris municipalities. I searched the registers, I interviewed two solicitors, I have seen all the documents. There is no doubt possible."

"But that does not explain the crime, or rather the series of crimes."

"Yes, it does," declared Lupin. "And, from the start, from the first hour when I meddled in this business, some words which Mlle. Darcieux used made me suspect that direction which my investigations must take. 'I was not quite five years old when my mother died,' she said. 'That was sixteen years ago.' Mlle. Darcieux, therefore, was nearly twenty-one, that is to say, she was on the verge of attaining her majority. I at once saw that this was an important detail. The day on which you reach your majority is the day on which your accounts are rendered. What was the financial position of Mlle. Darcieux, who was her mother's natural heiress? Of course, I did not think of the father for a second. To begin with, one can't imagine a thing like that; and then the farce which M. Darcieux was playing... helpless, bedridden, ill...."

"Really ill," interrupted the doctor.

"All this diverted suspicion from him... the more so as I believe that he himself was exposed to criminal attacks. But was there not in the family some person who would be interested in their removal? My journey to Paris revealed the truth to me: Mlle. Darcieux inherits a large fortune from her mother, of which her stepfather draws the income. The solicitor was to have called a meeting of the family in Paris next month. The truth would have been out. It meant ruin to M. Darcieux."

"Then he had put no money by?"

"Yes, but he had lost a great deal as the result of unfortunate speculations."

"But, after all, Jeanne would not have taken the management of her fortune out of his hands!"

"There is one detail which you do not know, doctor, and which I learnt from reading the torn letter. Mlle. Darcieux is in love with the brother of Marceline, her Versailles friend; M. Darcieux was opposed to the marriage; and—you now see the reason—she was waiting until she came of age to be married."

"You're right," said the doctor, "you're right.... It meant his ruin."

"His absolute ruin. One chance of saving himself remained, the death of his stepdaughter, of whom he is the next heir."

"Certainly, but on condition that no one suspected him."

"Of course; and that is why he contrived the series of accidents, so that the death might appear to be due to misadventure. And that is why I, on my side, wishing to bring things to a head, asked you to tell him of Mlle. Darcieux's impending departure. From that moment, it was no longer enough for the would-be sick man to wander about the grounds and the passages, in the dark, and execute some leisurely thought-out plan. No, he had to act, to act at once, without preparation, violently, dagger in hand. I had no doubt that he would decide to do it. And he did."

"Then he had no suspicions?"

"Of me, yes. He felt that I would return tonight, and he kept a watch at the place where I had already climbed the wall."

"Well?"

"Well," said Lupin, laughing, "I received a bullet full in the chest... or rather my pocketbook received a bullet.... Here, you can see the hole.... So I tumbled from the tree, like a dead man. Thinking that he was rid of his only adversary, he went back to the house. I saw him prowl about for two hours. Then, making up his mind, he went to the coach-house, took a ladder and set it against the window. I had only to follow him."

The doctor reflected and said:

"You could have collared him earlier. Why did you let him come up? It was a sore trial for Jeanne... and unnecessary."

"On the contrary, it was indispensable! Mlle. Darcieux would never have accepted the truth. It was essential that she should see the murderer's very face. You must tell her all the circumstances when she wakes. She will soon be well again."

"But... M. Darcieux?"

"You can explain his disappearance as you think best... a sudden journey... a fit of madness.... There will be a few inquiries.... And you may be sure that he will never be heard of again."

The doctor nodded his head:

"Yes... that is so... that is so... you are right. You have managed all this business with extraordinary skill; and Jeanne owes you her life. She will thank you in person.... But now, can I be of use to you in any way? You told me that you were connected with the detective-service.... Will you allow me to write and praise your conduct, your courage?"

Lupin began to laugh:

"Certainly! A letter of that kind will do me a world of good. You might write to my immediate superior, Chief-inspector Ganimard. He will be glad to hear that his favourite officer, Paul Daubreuil, of the Rue de Surène, has once again distinguished himself by a brilliant action. As it happens, I have an appointment to meet him about a case of which you may have heard: the case of the red scarf.... How pleased my dear M. Ganimard will be!"

VII

A Tragedy in the Forest of Morgues

The village was terror-stricken.

It was on a Sunday morning. The peasants of Saint-Nicolas and the neighbourhood were coming out of church and spreading across the square, when, suddenly, the women who were walking ahead and who had already turned into the highroad fell back with loud cries of dismay.

At the same moment, an enormous motorcar, looking like some appalling monster, came tearing into sight at a headlong rate of speed. Amid the shouts of the madly scattering people, it made straight for the church, swerved, just as it seemed about to dash itself to pieces against the steps, grazed the wall of the presbytery, regained the continuation of the national road, dashed along, turned the corner and disappeared, without, by some incomprehensible miracle, having so much as brushed against any of the persons crowding the square.

But they had seen! They had seen a man in the driver's seat, wrapped in a goatskin coat, with a fur cap on his head and his face disguised in a pair of large goggles, and, with him, on the front of that seat, flung back, bent in two, a woman whose head, all covered with blood, hung down over the bonnet....

And they had heard! They had heard the woman's screams, screams of horror, screams of agony....

And it was all such a vision of hell and carnage that the people stood, for some seconds, motionless, stupefied.

"Blood!" roared somebody.

There was blood everywhere, on the cobblestones of the square, on the ground hardened by the first frosts of autumn; and, when a number of men and boys rushed off in pursuit of the motor, they had but to take those sinister marks for their guide.

The marks, on their part, followed the highroad, but in a very strange manner, going from one side to the other and leaving a zigzag track, in the wake of the tires, that made those who saw it shudder. How was it that the car had not bumped against that tree? How had it been righted, instead of smashing into that bank? What novice, what madman, what drunkard, what frightened criminal was driving that motorcar with such astounding bounds and swerves?

One of the peasants declared:

"They will never do the turn in the forest."

And another said:

"Of course they won't! She's bound to upset!"

The Forest of Morgues began at half a mile beyond Saint-Nicolas; and the road, which was straight up to that point, except for a slight bend where it left the village, started climbing, immediately after entering the forest, and made an abrupt turn among the rocks and trees. No motorcar was able to take this turn without first slackening speed. There were posts to give notice of the danger.

The breathless peasants reached the quincunx of beeches that formed the edge of the forest. And one of them at once cried:

"There you are!"

"What?"

"Upset!"

The car, a limousine, had turned turtle and lay smashed, twisted and shapeless. Beside it, the woman's dead body. But the most horrible, sordid, stupefying thing was the woman's head, crushed, flattened, invisible under a block of stone, a huge block of stone lodged there by some unknown and prodigious agency. As for the man in the goatskin coat he was nowhere to be found.

He was not found on the scene of the accident. He was not found either in the neighbourhood. Moreover, some workmen coming down the Côte de Morgues declared that they had not seen anybody.

The man, therefore, had taken refuge in the woods.

The gendarmes, who were at once sent for, made a minute search, assisted by the peasants, but discovered nothing. In the same way, the examining-magistrates, after a close inquiry lasting for several days, found no clue capable of throwing the least light upon this inscrutable tragedy. On the contrary, the investigations only led to further mysteries and further improbabilities.

Thus it was ascertained that the block of stone came from where there had been a landslip, at least forty yards away. And the murderer, in a few minutes, had carried it all that distance and flung it on his victim's head.

On the other hand, the murderer, who was most certainly not hiding in the forest—for, if so, he must inevitably have been discovered, the forest being of limited extent—had the audacity, eight days after the crime, to come back to the turn on the hill and leave his goatskin coat there. Why? With what object? There was nothing in the pockets of the coat, except a corkscrew and a napkin. What did it all mean?

Inquiries were made of the builder of the motorcar, who recognized the limousine as one which he had sold, three years ago, to a Russian. The said Russian, declared the manufacturer, had sold it again at once. To whom? No one knew. The car bore no number.

Then again, it was impossible to identify the dead woman's body. Her clothes and underclothing were not marked in any way. And the face was quite unknown.

Meanwhile, detectives were going along the national road in the direction opposite to that taken by the actors in this mysterious tragedy. But who was to prove that the car had followed that particular road on the previous night?

They examined every yard of the ground, they questioned everybody. At last, they succeeded in learning that, on the Saturday evening, a limousine had stopped outside a grocer's shop in a small town situated about two hundred miles from Saint-Nicolas, on a highway branching out of the national road. The driver had first filled his tank, bought some spare cans of petrol and lastly taken away a small stock of provisions: a ham, fruit, biscuits, wine and a half-bottle of Three Star brandy.

There was a lady on the driver's seat. She did not get down. The blinds of the limousine were drawn. One of these blinds was seen to move several times. The shopman was positive that there was somebody inside.

Presuming the shopman's evidence to be correct, then the problem became even more complicated, for, so far, no clue had revealed the presence of a third person.

Meanwhile, as the travellers had supplied themselves with provisions, it remained to be discovered what they had done with them and what had become of the remains.

The detectives retraced their steps. It was not until they came to the fork of the two roads, at a spot eleven or twelve miles from Saint-Nicolas, that they met a shepherd who, in answer to their questions, directed them to a neighbouring field, hidden from view behind the screen of bushes, where he had seen an empty bottle and other things.

The detectives were convinced at the first examination. The motorcar had stopped there; and the unknown travellers, probably after a night's rest in their car, had breakfasted and resumed their journey in the course of the morning.

One unmistakable proof was the half-bottle of Three Star brandy sold by the grocer. This bottle had its neck broken clean off with a stone. The stone employed for the purpose was picked up, as was the neck of the bottle, with its cork, covered with a tinfoil seal. The seal showed marks of attempts that had been made to uncork the bottle in the ordinary manner.

The detectives continued their search and followed a ditch that ran along the field at right angles to the road. It ended in a little spring, hidden under brambles, which seemed to emit an offensive smell. On lifting the brambles, they perceived a corpse, the corpse of a man whose head had been smashed in, so that it formed little more than a sort of pulp, swarming with vermin. The body was dressed in jacket and trousers of dark-brown leather. The pockets were empty: no papers, no pocketbook, no watch.

The grocer and his shopman were summoned and, two days later, formally identified, by his dress and figure, the traveller who had bought the petrol and provisions on the Saturday evening.

The whole case, therefore, had to be reopened on a fresh basis. The authorities were confronted with a tragedy no longer enacted by two persons, a man and a woman, of whom one had killed the other, but by three persons, including two victims, of whom one was the very man who was accused of killing his companion.

As to the murderer, there was no doubt: he was the person who travelled inside the motorcar and who took the precaution to remain concealed behind the curtains. He had first got rid of the driver and rifled his pockets and then, after wounding the woman, carried her off in a mad dash for death.

Given a fresh case, unexpected discoveries, unforeseen evidence, one might have hoped that the mystery would be cleared up, or, at least, that the inquiry would point a few steps along the road to the truth. But not at all. The corpse was simply placed beside the first corpse. New problems were added to the old. The accusation of murder was shifted from the one to the other. And there it ended. Outside those tangible, obvious facts there was nothing but darkness. The name of the woman, the name of the man, the name of the murderer were so many riddles. And then what had become of the murderer? If he had disappeared from one moment to the other, that in itself would have been a tolerably curious phenomenon. But the phenomenon was actually something very like a miracle, inasmuch as the murderer had not absolutely disappeared. He was there! He made a practice of returning to the scene of the catastrophe! In addition to the goatskin coat, a fur cap was picked up one day; and, by way of an unparalleled prodigy, one morning, after a whole night spent on guard in the rock, beside the famous turning, the detectives found, on the grass of the turning itself, a pair of motor-goggles, broken, rusty, dirty, done for. How had the murderer managed to bring back those goggles unseen by the detectives? And, above all, why had he brought them back?

Men's brains reeled in the presence of such abnormalities. They were almost afraid to pursue the ambiguous adventure. They received the impression of a heavy, stifling, breathless atmosphere, which dimmed the eyes and baffled the most clear-sighted.

The magistrate in charge of the case fell ill. Four days later, his successor confessed that the matter was beyond him.

Two tramps were arrested and at once released. Another was pursued, but not caught; moreover, there was no evidence of any sort or kind against him. In short, it was nothing but one helpless muddle of mist and contradiction.

An accident, the merest accident led to the solution, or rather produced a series of circumstances that ended by leading to the solution. A reporter on the staff of an important Paris paper, who had been sent to make investigations on the spot, concluded his article with the following words:

"I repeat, therefore, that we must wait for fresh events, fresh facts; we must wait for some lucky accident. As things stand, we are simply wasting our time. The elements of truth are not even sufficient to suggest a plausible theory. We are in the midst of the most absolute, painful, impenetrable darkness. There is nothing to be done. All the Sherlock Holmeses in the world would not know what to make of the mystery, and Arsène Lupin himself, if he will allow me to say so, would have to pay forfeit here."

On the day after the appearance of that article, the newspaper in question printed this telegram:

"Have sometimes paid forfeit, but never over such a silly thing as this. The Saint-Nicolas tragedy is a mystery for babies.

"ARSÈNE LUPIN."

And the editor added:

"We insert this telegram as a matter of curiosity, for it is obviously the work of a wag. Arsène Lupin, past-master though he be in the art of practical joking, would be the last man to display such childish flippancy."

Two days elapsed; and then the paper published the famous letter, so precise and categorical in its conclusions, in which Arsène Lupin furnished the solution of the problem. I quote it in full:

"SIR:

"You have taken me on my weak side by defying me. You challenge me, and I accept the challenge. And I will begin by declaring once more that the Saint-Nicolas tragedy is a mystery for babies. I know nothing so simple, so natural; and the proof of the simplicity shall lie in the succinctness of my demonstration. It is contained in these few words: when a crime seems to go beyond the ordinary scope of things, when it seems unusual and stupid, then there are many chances that its explanation is to be found in superordinary, supernatural, superhuman motives.

"I say that there are many chances, for we must always allow for the part played by absurdity in the most logical and commonplace events. But, of course, it is impossible to see things as they are and not to take account of the absurd and the disproportionate.

"I was struck from the very beginning by that very evident character of unusualness. We have, first of all, the awkward, zigzag course of the motorcar, which would give one the impression that the car was driven by a novice. People have spoken of a drunkard or a madman, a justifiable supposition in itself. But neither madness nor drunkenness would account for the incredible strength required to transport, especially in so short a space of time, the stone with which the unfortunate woman's head was crushed. That proceeding called for a muscular power so great that I do not hesitate to look upon it as a second sign of the unusualness that marks the whole tragedy. And why move that enormous stone, to finish off the victim, when a mere pebble would have done the work? Why again was the murderer not killed, or at least reduced to a temporary state of helplessness, in the terrible somersault turned by the car? How did he disappear? And why, having disappeared, did he return to the scene of the accident? Why did he throw his fur coat there; then, on another day, his cap; then, on another day, his goggles?

"Unusual, useless, stupid acts.

"Why, besides, convey that wounded, dying woman on the driver's seat of the car, where everybody could see her? Why do that, instead of putting her inside, or flinging her into some corner, dead, just as the man was flung under the brambles in the ditch?

"Unusualness, stupidity.

"Everything in the whole story is absurd. Everything points to hesitation, incoherency, awkwardness, the silliness of a child or rather of a mad, blundering savage, of a brute.

"Look at the bottle of brandy. There was a corkscrew: it was found in the pocket of the great coat. Did the murderer use it? Yes, the marks of the corkscrew can be seen on the seal. But the operation was too complicated for him. He broke the neck with a stone. Always stones: observe that detail. They are the only weapon, the only implement which the creature employs. It is his customary weapon, his familiar implement. He kills the man with a stone, he kills the woman with a stone and he opens bottles with a stone!

"A brute, I repeat, a savage; disordered, unhinged, suddenly driven mad. By what? Why, of course, by that same brandy, which he swallowed at a draught while the driver and his companion were having breakfast in the field. He got out of the limousine, in which he was travelling, in his goatskin coat and his fur cap, took the bottle, broke off the neck and drank. There is the whole story. Having drunk, he went raving mad and hit out at random, without reason. Then, seized with instinctive fear, dreading the inevitable punishment, he hid the body of the man. Then, like an idiot, he took up the wounded woman and ran away. He ran away in that motorcar which he did not know how to work, but which to him represented safety, escape from capture.

"But the money, you will ask, the stolen pocketbook? Why, who says that he was the thief? Who says that it was not some passing tramp, some labourer, guided by the stench of the corpse?

"Very well, you object, but the brute would have been found, as he is hiding somewhere near the turn, and as, after all, he must eat and drink.

"Well, well, I see that you have not yet understood. The simplest way, I suppose, to have done and to answer your objections is to make straight for the mark. Then let the gentlemen of the police and the gendarmerie themselves make straight for the mark. Let them take firearms. Let them explore the forest within a radius of two or three hundred yards from the turn, no more. But, instead of exploring with their heads down and their eyes fixed on the ground, let them look up into the air, yes, into the air, among the leaves and branches of the tallest oaks and the most unlikely beeches. And, believe me, they will see him. For he is there. He is there, bewildered, piteously at a loss, seeking for the man and woman whom he has killed, looking for them and waiting for them and not daring to go away and quite unable to understand.

"I myself am exceedingly sorry that I am kept in town by urgent private affairs and by some complicated matters of business which I have to set going, for I should much have liked to see the end of this rather curious adventure.

"Pray, therefore excuse me to my kind friends in the police and permit me to be, sir,

"Your obedient servant,
"ARSÈNE LUPIN."

The upshot will be remembered. The "gentlemen of the police and the gendarmerie" shrugged their shoulders and paid no attention to this lucubration. But four of the local country gentry took their rifles and went shooting, with their eyes fixed skyward, as though they meant to pot a few rooks. In half an hour they had caught sight of the murderer. Two shots, and he came tumbling from bough to bough. He was only wounded, and they took him alive.

That evening, a Paris paper, which did not yet know of the capture, printed the following paragraphs:

"Enquiries are being made after a M. and Mme. Bragoff, who landed at Marseilles six weeks ago and there hired a motorcar. They had been living in Australia for many years, during which time they had not visited Europe; and they wrote to the director of the Jardin d'Acclimatation, with whom they were in the habit of corresponding, that they were bringing with them a curious creature, of an entirely unknown species, of which it was difficult to say whether it was a man or a monkey.

"According to M. Bragoff, who is an eminent archæologist, the specimen in question is the anthropoid ape, or rather the ape-man, the existence of which had not hitherto been definitely proved. The structure is said to be exactly similar to that of *Pithecanthropus erectus*, discovered by Dr. Dubois in Java in 1891.

"This curious, intelligent and observant animal acted as its owner's servant on their property in Australia and used to clean their motorcar and even attempt to drive it.

"The question that is being asked is where are M. and Mme. Bragoff? Where is the strange primate that landed with them at Marseilles?"

The answer to this question was now made easy. Thanks to the hints supplied by Arsène Lupin, all the elements of the tragedy were known. Thanks to him, the culprit was in the hands of the law.

You can see him at the Jardin d'Acclimatation, where he is locked up under the name of "Three Stars." He is, in point of fact, a monkey; but he is also a man. He has the gentleness and the wisdom of the domestic animals and the sadness which they feel when their master dies. But he has many other qualities that bring him much closer to humanity: he is treacherous, cruel, idle, greedy and quarrelsome; and, above all, he is immoderately fond of brandy.

Apart from that, he is a monkey. Unless indeed...!

A few days after Three Stars' arrest, I saw Arsène Lupin standing in front of his cage. Lupin was manifestly trying to solve this interesting problem for himself. I at once said, for I had set my heart upon having the matter out with him:

"You know, Lupin, that intervention of yours, your argument, your letter, in short, did not surprise me so much as you might think!"

"Oh, really?" he said, calmly. "And why?"

"Why? Because the incident has occurred before, seventy or eighty years ago. Edgar Allan Poe made it the subject of one of his finest tales. In those circumstances, the key to the riddle was easy enough to find."

Arsène Lupin took my arm, and walking away with me, said:

"When did you guess it, yourself?"

"On reading your letter," I confessed.

"And at what part of my letter?"

"At the end."

"At the end, eh? After I had dotted all the *i*'s. So here is a crime which accident causes to be repeated, under quite different conditions, it is true, but still with the same sort of hero; and your eyes had to be opened, as well as other people's. It needed the assistance of my letter, the letter in which I amused myself—apart from the exigencies of the facts—by employing the argument and sometimes the identical words used by the American poet in a story which everybody has read. So you see that my letter was not absolutely useless and that one may safely venture to repeat to people things which they have learnt only to forget them."

Wherewith Lupin turned on his heel and burst out laughing in the face of an old monkey, who sat with the air of a philosopher, gravely meditating.

VIII

LUPIN'S MARRIAGE

"Monsieur Arsène Lupin has the honour to inform you of his approaching marriage with Mademoiselle Angélique de Sarzeau-Vendôme, Princesse de Bourbon-Condé, and to request the pleasure of your company at the wedding, which will take place at the church of Sainte-Clotilde...."

"The Duc de Sarzeau-Vendôme has the honour to inform you of the approaching marriage of his daughter Angélique, Princesse de Bourbon-Condé, with Monsieur Arsène Lupin, and to request...."

Jean Duc de Sarzeau-Vendôme could not finish reading the invitations which he held in his trembling hand. Pale with anger, his long, lean body shaking with tremors:

"There!" he gasped, handing the two communications to his daughter. "This is what our friends have received! This has been the talk of Paris since yesterday! What do you say to that dastardly insult, Angélique? What would your poor mother say to it, if she were alive?"

Angélique was tall and thin like her father, skinny and angular like him. She was thirty-three years of age, always dressed in black stuff, shy and retiring in manner, with a head too small in proportion to her height and narrowed on either side until the nose seemed to jut forth in protest against such parsimony. And yet it would be impossible to say that she was ugly, for her eyes were extremely beautiful, soft and grave, proud and a little sad: pathetic eyes which to see once was to remember.

She flushed with shame at hearing her father's words, which told her the scandal of which she was the victim. But, as she loved him, notwithstanding his harshness to her, his injustice and despotism, she said:

"Oh, I think it must be meant for a joke, father, to which we need pay no attention!"

"A joke? Why, everyone is gossiping about it! A dozen papers have printed the confounded notice this morning, with satirical comments. They quote our pedigree, our ancestors, our illustrious dead. They pretend to take the thing seriously...."

"Still, no one could believe...."

"Of course not. But that doesn't prevent us from being the byword of Paris."

"It will all be forgotten by tomorrow."

"Tomorrow, my girl, people will remember that the name of Angélique de Sarzeau-Vendôme has been bandied about as it should not be. Oh, if I could find out the name of the scoundrel who has dared...."

At that moment, Hyacinthe, the duke's valet, came in and said that monsieur le duc was wanted on the telephone. Still fuming, he took down the receiver and growled:

"Well? Who is it? Yes, it's the Duc de Sarzeau-Vendôme speaking."

A voice replied:

"I want to apologize to you, monsieur le duc, and to Mlle. Angélique. It's my secretary's fault."

"Your secretary?"

"Yes, the invitations were only a rough draft which I meant to submit to you. Unfortunately my secretary thought...."

"But, tell me, monsieur, who are you?"

"What, monsieur le duc, don't you know my voice? The voice of your future son-in-law?"

"What!"

"Arsène Lupin."

The duke dropped into a chair. His face was livid.

"Arsène Lupin... it's he... Arsène Lupin...."

Angélique gave a smile:

"You see, father, it's only a joke, a hoax."

But the duke's rage broke out afresh and he began to walk up and down, moving his arms:

"I shall go to the police!... The fellow can't be allowed to make a fool of me in this way!... If there's any law left in the land, it must be stopped!"

Hyacinthe entered the room again. He brought two visiting-cards.

"Chotois? Lepetit? Don't know them."

"They are both journalists, monsieur le duc."

"What do they want?"

"They would like to speak to monsieur le duc with regard to... the marriage...."

"Turn them out!" exclaimed the duke. "Kick them out! And tell the porter not to admit scum of that sort to my house in future."

"Please, father..." Angélique ventured to say.

"As for you, shut up! If you had consented to marry one of your cousins when I wanted you to this wouldn't have happened."

The same evening, one of the two reporters printed, on the front page of his paper, a somewhat fanciful story of his expedition to the family mansion of the Sarzeau-Vendômes, in the Rue de Varennes, and expatiated pleasantly upon the old nobleman's wrathful protests.

The next morning, another newspaper published an interview with Arsène Lupin which was supposed to have taken place in a lobby at the Opera. Arsène Lupin retorted in a letter to the editor:

"I share my prospective father-in-law's indignation to the full. The sending out of the invitations was a gross breach of etiquette for which I am not responsible, but for which I wish to make a public apology. Why, sir, the date of the marriage is not yet fixed. My bride's father suggests early in May. She and I think that six weeks is really too long to wait!..."

That which gave a special piquancy to the affair and added immensely to the enjoyment of the friends of the family was the duke's well-known character: his pride and the uncompromising nature of his ideas and principles. Duc Jean was the last descendant of the Barons de Sarzeau, the most ancient family in Brittany; he was the lineal descendant of that Sarzeau who, upon marrying a Vendôme, refused to bear the new title which

Louis XV forced upon him until after he had been imprisoned for ten years in the Bastille; and he had abandoned none of the prejudices of the old regime. In his youth, he followed the Comte de Chambord into exile. In his old age, he refused a seat in the Chamber on the pretext that a Sarzeau could only sit with his peers.

The incident stung him to the quick. Nothing could pacify him. He cursed Lupin in good round terms, threatened him with every sort of punishment and rounded on his daughter:

"There, if you had only married!... After all you had plenty of chances. Your three cousins, Mussy, d'Emboise and Caorches, are noblemen of good descent, allied to the best families, fairly well-off; and they are still anxious to marry you. Why do you refuse them? Ah, because miss is a dreamer, a sentimentalist; and because her cousins are too fat, or too thin, or too coarse for her...."

She was, in fact, a dreamer. Left to her own devices from childhood, she had read all the books of chivalry, all the colourless romances of olden-time that littered the ancestral presses; and she looked upon life as a fairytale in which the beauteous maidens are always happy, while the others wait till death for the bridegroom who does not come. Why should she marry one of her cousins when they were only after her money, the millions which she had inherited from her mother? She might as well remain an old maid and go on dreaming....

She answered, gently:

"You will end by making yourself ill, father. Forget this silly business."

But how could he forget it? Every morning, some pinprick renewed his wound. Three days running, Angélique received a wonderful sheaf of flowers, with Arsène Lupin's card peeping from it. The duke could not go to his club but a friend accosted him:

"That was a good one today!"

"What was?"

"Why, your son-in-law's latest! Haven't you seen it? Here, read it for yourself: 'M. Arsène Lupin is petitioning the Council of State for permission to add his wife's name to his own and to be known henceforth as Lupin de Sarzeau-Vendôme.'"

And, the next day, he read:

"As the young bride, by virtue of an unrepealed decree of Charles X, bears the title and arms of the Bourbon-Condés, of whom she is the heiress-of-line, the eldest son of the Lupins de Sarzeau-Vendôme will be styled Prince de Bourbon-Condé."

And, the day after, an advertisement.

"Exhibition of Mlle. de Sarzeau-Vendôme's trousseau at Messrs. ————'s Great Linen Warehouse. Each article marked with initials L. S. V."

Then an illustrated paper published a photographic scene: the duke, his daughter and his son-in-law sitting at a table playing three-handed auction-bridge.

And the date also was announced with a great flourish of trumpets: the 4th of May.

And particulars were given of the marriage-settlement. Lupin showed himself wonderfully disinterested. He was prepared to sign, the newspapers said, with his eyes closed, without knowing the figure of the dowry.

All these things drove the old duke crazy. His hatred of Lupin assumed morbid proportions. Much as it went against the grain, he called on the prefect of police, who advised him to be on his guard:

"We know the gentleman's ways; he is employing one of his favourite dodges. Forgive the expression, monsieur le duc, but he is 'nursing' you. Don't fall into the trap."

"What dodge? What trap?" asked the duke, anxiously.

"He is trying to make you lose your head and to lead you, by intimidation, to do something which you would refuse to do in cold blood."

"Still, M. Arsène Lupin can hardly hope that I will offer him my daughter's hand!"

"No, but he hopes that you will commit, to put it mildly, a blunder."

"What blunder?"

"Exactly that blunder which he wants you to commit."

"Then you think, *monsieur le préfet*…?"

"I think the best thing you can do, monsieur le duc, is to go home, or, if all this excitement worries you, to run down to the country and stay there quietly, without upsetting yourself."

This conversation only increased the old duke's fears. Lupin appeared to him in the light of a terrible person, who employed diabolical methods and kept accomplices in every sphere of society. Prudence was the watchword.

And life, from that moment, became intolerable. The duke grew more crabbed and silent than ever and denied his door to all his old friends and even to Angélique's three suitors, her Cousins de Mussy, d'Emboise and de Caorches, who were none of them on speaking terms with the others, in consequence of their rivalry, and who were in the habit of calling, turn and turn about, every week.

For no earthly reason, he dismissed his butler and his coachman. But he dared not fill their places, for fear of engaging creatures of Arsène Lupin's; and his own man, Hyacinthe, in whom he had every confidence, having had him in his service for over forty years, had to take upon himself the laborious duties of the stables and the pantry.

"Come, father," said Angélique, trying to make him listen to common sense. "I really can't see what you are afraid of. No one can force me into this ridiculous marriage."

"Well, of course, that's not what I'm afraid of."

"What then, father?"

"How can I tell? An abduction! A burglary! An act of violence! There is no doubt that the villain is scheming something; and there is also no doubt that we are surrounded by spies."

One afternoon, he received a newspaper in which the following paragraph was marked in red pencil:

"The signing of the marriage-contract is fixed for this evening, at the Sarzeau-Vendôme town-house. It will be quite a private ceremony and only a few privileged friends will be present to congratulate the happy pair. The witnesses to the contract on behalf of Mlle. de Sarzeau-Vendôme, the Prince de la Rochefoucauld-Limours and the Comte de Chartres, will be introduced by M. Arsène Lupin to the two gentlemen who have claimed the honour of acting as his groomsmen, namely, the prefect of police and the governor of the Santé Prison."

Ten minutes later, the duke sent his servant Hyacinthe to the post with three express messages. At four o'clock, in Angélique's presence, he saw the three cousins: Mussy, fat, heavy, pasty-faced; d'Emboise, slender, fresh-coloured and shy: Caorches, short, thin and unhealthy-looking: all three, old bachelors by this time, lacking distinction in dress or appearance.

The meeting was a short one. The duke had worked out his whole plan of campaign, a defensive campaign, of which he set forth the first stage in explicit terms:

"Angélique and I will leave Paris tonight for our place in Brittany. I rely on you, my three nephews, to help us get away. You, d'Emboise, will come and fetch us in your car, with the hood up. You, Mussy, will bring your big motor and kindly see to the luggage with Hyacinthe, my man. You, Caorches, will go to the Gare d'Orléans and book our berths in the sleeping-car for Vannes by the 10:40 train. Is that settled?"

The rest of the day passed without incident. The duke, to avoid any accidental indiscretion, waited until after dinner to tell Hyacinthe to pack a trunk and a portmanteau. Hyacinthe was to accompany them, as well as Angélique's maid.

At nine o'clock, all the other servants went to bed, by their master's order. At ten minutes to ten, the duke, who was completing his preparations, heard the sound of a motor-horn. The porter opened the gates of the courtyard. The duke, standing at the window, recognized d'Emboise's landaulette:

"Tell him I shall be down presently," he said to Hyacinthe, "and let mademoiselle know."

In a few minutes, as Hyacinthe did not return, he left his room. But he was attacked on the landing by two masked men, who gagged and bound him before he could utter a cry. And one of the men said to him, in a low voice:

"Take this as a first warning, monsieur le duc. If you persist in leaving Paris and refusing your consent, it will be a more serious matter."

And the same man said to his companion:

"Keep an eye on him. I will see to the young lady."

By that time, two other confederates had secured the lady's maid; and Angélique, herself gagged, lay fainting on a couch in her boudoir.

She came to almost immediately, under the stimulus of a bottle of salts held to her nostrils; and, when she opened her eyes, she saw bending over her a young man, in evening-clothes, with a smiling and friendly face, who said:

"I implore your forgiveness, mademoiselle. All these happenings are a trifle sudden and this behaviour rather out of the way. But circumstances often compel us to deeds of which our conscience does not approve. Pray pardon me."

He took her hand very gently and slipped a broad gold ring on the girl's finger, saying:

"There, now we are engaged. Never forget the man who gave you this ring. He entreats you not to run away from him... and to stay in Paris and await the proofs of his devotion. Have faith in him."

He said all this in so serious and respectful a voice, with so much authority and deference, that she had not the strength to resist. Their eyes met. He whispered:

"The exquisite purity of your eyes! It would be heavenly to live with those eyes upon one. Now close them...."

He withdrew. His accomplices followed suit. The car drove off, and the house in the Rue de Varennes remained still and silent until the moment when Angélique, regaining complete consciousness, called out for the servants.

They found the duke, Hyacinthe, the lady's maid and the porter and his wife all tightly bound. A few priceless ornaments had disappeared, as well as the duke's pocketbook and all his jewellery; tie pins, pearl studs, watch and so on.

The police were advised without delay. In the morning it appeared that, on the evening before, d'Emboise, when leaving his house in the motorcar, was stabbed by his own chauffeur and thrown, half-dead, into a deserted street. Mussy and Caorches had each received a telephone-message, purporting to come from the duke, countermanding their attendance.

Next week, without troubling further about the police investigation, without obeying the summons of the examining-magistrate, without even reading Arsène Lupin's letters to the papers on "the Varennes Flight," the duke, his daughter and his valet stealthily took a slow train for Vannes and arrived one evening, at the old feudal castle that towers over the headland of Sarzeau. The duke at once organized a defence with the aid of the Breton peasants, true medieval vassals to a man. On the fourth day, Mussy arrived; on the fifth, Caorches; and, on the seventh, d'Emboise, whose wound was not as severe as had been feared.

The duke waited two days longer before communicating to those about him what, now that his escape had succeeded in spite of Lupin, he called the second part of his plan. He did so, in the presence of the three cousins, by a dictatorial order to Angélique, expressed in these peremptory terms:

"All this bother is upsetting me terribly. I have entered on a struggle with this man whose daring you have seen for yourself; and the struggle is killing me. I want to end it at all costs. There is only one way of doing so, Angélique, and that is for you to release me from all responsibility by accepting the hand of one of your cousins. Before a month is out, you must be the wife of Mussy, Caorches or d'Emboise. You have a free choice. Make your decision."

For four whole days Angélique wept and entreated her father, but in vain. She felt that he would be inflexible and that she must end by submitting to his wishes. She accepted:

"Whichever you please, father. I love none of them. So I may as well be unhappy with one as with the other."

Thereupon a fresh discussion ensued, as the duke wanted to compel her to make her own choice. She stood firm. Reluctantly and for financial considerations, he named d'Emboise.

The banns were published without delay.

From that moment, the watch in and around the castle was increased twofold, all the more inasmuch as Lupin's silence and the sudden cessation of the campaign which he had been conducting in the press could not but alarm the Duc de Sarzeau-Vendôme. It was obvious that the enemy was getting ready to strike and would endeavour to oppose the marriage by one of his characteristic moves.

Nevertheless, nothing happened: nothing two days before the ceremony, nothing on the day before, nothing on the morning itself. The marriage took place in the mayor's office, followed by the religious celebration in church; and the thing was done.

Then and not till then, the duke breathed freely. Notwithstanding his daughter's sadness, notwithstanding the embarrassed silence of his son-in-law, who found the situation a little trying, he rubbed his hands with an air of pleasure, as though he had achieved a brilliant victory:

"Tell them to lower the drawbridge," he said to Hyacinthe, "and to admit everybody. We have nothing more to fear from that scoundrel."

After the wedding-breakfast, he had wine served out to the peasants and clinked glasses with them. They danced and sang.

At three o'clock, he returned to the ground-floor rooms. It was the hour for his afternoon nap. He walked to the guardroom at the end of the suite. But he had no sooner placed his foot on the threshold than he stopped suddenly and exclaimed:

"What are you doing here, d'Emboise? Is this a joke?"

D'Emboise was standing before him, dressed as a Breton fisherman, in a dirty jacket and breeches, torn, patched and many sizes too large for him.

The duke seemed dumbfounded. He stared with eyes of amazement at that face which he knew and which, at the same time, roused memories of a very distant past within his brain. Then he strode abruptly to one of the windows overlooking the castle-terrace and called:

"Angélique!"

"What is it, father?" she asked, coming forward.

"Where's your husband?"

"Over there, father," said Angélique, pointing to d'Emboise, who was smoking a cigarette and reading, some way off.

The duke stumbled and fell into a chair, with a great shudder of fright:

"Oh, I shall go mad!"

But the man in the fisherman's garb knelt down before him and said:

"Look at me, uncle. You know me, don't you? I'm your nephew, the one who used to play here in the old days, the one whom you called Jacquot.... Just think a minute.... Here, look at this scar...."

"Yes, yes," stammered the duke, "I recognize you. It's Jacques. But the other one...."
He put his hands to his head:

"And yet, no, it can't be... Explain yourself.... I don't understand.... I don't want to understand...."

There was a pause, during which the newcomer shut the window and closed the door leading to the next room. Then he came up to the old duke, touched him gently on the shoulder, to wake him from his torpor, and without further preface, as though to cut short any explanation that was not absolutely necessary, spoke as follows:

"Four years ago, that is to say, in the eleventh year of my voluntary exile, when I settled in the extreme south of Algeria, I made the acquaintance, in the course of a hunting-expedition arranged by a big Arab chief, of a man whose geniality, whose charm of manner, whose consummate prowess, whose indomitable pluck, whose combined humour and depth of mind fascinated me in the highest degree. The Comte d'Andrésy spent six weeks as my guest. After he left, we kept up a correspondence at regular intervals. I also often saw his name in the papers, in the society and sporting columns. He was to come back and I was preparing to receive him, three months ago, when, one evening as I was out riding, my two Arab attendants flung themselves upon me, bound me, blindfolded me and took me, travelling day and night, for a week, along deserted roads, to a bay on the coast, where five men awaited them. I was at once carried on board a small steam-yacht, which weighed anchor without delay. There was nothing to tell me who the men were nor what their object was in kidnapping me. They had locked me into a narrow cabin, secured by a massive door and lighted by a porthole protected arrival. I learnt that Angélique's marriage was celebrated this morning."

The old duke had not spoken a word. With his eyes riveted on the stranger's, he was listening in ever-increasing dismay. At times, the thought of the warnings given him by the prefect of police returned to his mind:

"They're nursing you, monsieur le duc, they are nursing you."

He said, in a hollow voice:

"Speak on... finish your story.... All this is ghastly.... I don't understand it yet... and I feel nervous...."

The stranger resumed:

"I am sorry to say, the story is easily pieced together and is summed up in a few sentences. It is like this: the Comte d'Andrésy remembered several things from his stay with me and from the confidences which I was foolish enough to make to him. First of all, I was your nephew and yet you had seen comparatively little of me, because I left Sarzeau when I was quite a child, and since then our intercourse was limited to the few weeks which I spent here, fifteen years ago, when I proposed for the hand of my Cousin Angélique; secondly, having broken with the past, I received no letters; lastly, there was a certain physical resemblance between d'Andrésy and myself which could be accentuated to such an extent as to become striking. His scheme was built up on those three points. He bribed my Arab servants to give him warning in case I left Algeria. Then he went back to Paris, bearing my name and made up to look exactly like me, came to see you, was invited to your house once a fortnight and lived under my name, which thus became one of the many aliases beneath which he conceals his real identity. Three months ago, when 'the apple was ripe,' as he says in his letters, he began the attack by a series of communications to the press; and, at the same time, fearing no doubt that some newspaper would tell me in Algeria the part that was being played under my name in Paris, he had me assaulted by my servants and kidnapped by his confederates. I need not explain any more in so far as you are concerned, uncle."

The Duc de Sarzeau-Vendôme was shaken with a fit of nervous trembling. The awful truth to which he refused to open his eyes appeared to him in its nakedness and assumed the hateful countenance of the enemy. He clutched his nephew's hands and said to him, fiercely, despairingly:

"It's Lupin, is it not?"

"Yes, uncle."

"And it's to him... it's to him that I have given my daughter!"

"Yes, uncle, to him, who has stolen my name of Jacques d'Emboise from me and stolen your daughter from you. Angélique is the wedded wife of Arsène Lupin; and that in accordance with your orders. This letter in his handwriting bears witness to it. He has upset your whole life, thrown you off your balance, besieging your hours of waking and your nights of dreaming, rifling your town-house, until the moment when, seized with terror, you took refuge here, where, thinking that you would escape his artifices and his rapacity, you told your daughter to choose one of her three cousins, Mussy, d'Emboise or Caorches, as her husband."

"But why did she select that one rather than the others?"

"It was you who selected him, uncle."

"At random... because he had the biggest income...."

"No, not at random, but on the insidious, persistent and very clever advice of your servant Hyacinthe."

The duke gave a start:

"What! Is Hyacinthe an accomplice?"

"No, not of Arsène Lupin, but of the man whom he believes to be d'Emboise and who promised to give him a hundred thousand francs within a week after the marriage."

"Oh, the villain!... He planned everything, foresaw everything...."

"Foresaw everything, uncle, down to shamming an attempt upon his life so as to avert suspicion, down to shamming a wound received in your service."

"But with what object? Why all these dastardly tricks?"

"Angélique has a fortune of eleven million francs. Your solicitor in Paris was to hand the securities next week to the counterfeit d'Emboise, who had only to realize them forthwith and disappear. But, this very morning, you yourself were to hand your son-in-law, as a personal wedding-present, five hundred thousand francs' worth of bearer-stock, which he has arranged to deliver to one of his accomplices at nine o'clock this evening, outside the castle, near the Great Oak, so that they may be negotiated tomorrow morning in Brussels."

The Duc de Sarzeau-Vendôme had risen from his seat and was stamping furiously up and down the room:

"At nine o'clock this evening?" he said. "We'll see about that.... We'll see about that.... I'll have the gendarmes here before then...."

"Arsène Lupin laughs at gendarmes."

"Let's telegraph to Paris."

"Yes, but how about the five hundred thousand francs?... And, still worse, uncle, the scandal?... Think of this: your daughter, Angélique de Sarzeau-Vendôme, married to that swindler, that thief.... No, no, it would never do...."

"What then?"

"What?..."

The nephew now rose and, stepping to a gun-rack, took down a rifle and laid it on the table, in front of the duke:

"Away in Algeria, uncle, on the verge of the desert, when we find ourselves face to face with a wild beast, we do not send for the gendarmes. We take our rifle and we shoot the wild beast. Otherwise, the beast would tear us to pieces with its claws."

"What do you mean?"

"I mean that, over there, I acquired the habit of dispensing with the gendarmes. It is a rather summary way of doing justice, but it is the best way, believe me, and today, in the present case, it is the only way. Once the beast is killed, you and I will bury it in some corner, unseen and unknown."

"And Angélique?"

"We will tell her later."

"What will become of her?"

"She will be my wife, the wife of the real d'Emboise. I desert her tomorrow and return to Algeria. The divorce will be granted in two months' time."

The duke listened, pale and staring, with set jaws. He whispered:

"Are you sure that his accomplices on the yacht will not inform him of your escape?"

"Not before tomorrow."

"So that...?"

"So that inevitably, at nine o'clock this evening, Arsène Lupin, on his way to the Great Oak, will take the patrol-path that follows the old ramparts and skirts the ruins of the chapel. I shall be there, in the ruins."

"I shall be there too," said the Duc de Sarzeau-Vendôme, quietly, taking down a gun.

It was now five o'clock. The duke talked some time longer to his nephew, examined the weapons, loaded them with fresh cartridges. Then, when night came, he took d'Emboise through the dark passages to his bedroom and hid him in an adjoining closet.

Nothing further happened until dinner. The duke forced himself to keep calm during the meal. From time to time, he stole a glance at his son-in-law and was surprised at the likeness between him and the real d'Emboise. It was the same complexion, the same cast of features, the same cut of hair. Nevertheless, the look of the eye was different, keener in this case and brighter; and gradually the duke discovered minor details which had passed unperceived till then and which proved the fellow's imposture.

The party broke up after dinner. It was eight o'clock. The duke went to his room and released his nephew. Ten minutes later, under cover of the darkness, they slipped into the ruins, gun in hand.

Meanwhile, Angélique, accompanied by her husband, had gone to the suite of rooms which she occupied on the ground-floor of a tower that flanked the left wing. Her husband stopped at the entrance to the rooms and said:

"I am going for a short stroll, Angélique. May I come to you here, when I return?"

"Yes," she replied.

He left her and went up to the first floor, which had been assigned to him as his quarters. The moment he was alone, he locked the door, noiselessly opened a window that looked over the landscape and leant out. He saw a shadow at the foot of the tower, some hundred feet or more below him. He whistled and received a faint whistle in reply.

He then took from a cupboard a thick leather satchel, crammed with papers, wrapped it in a piece of black cloth and tied it up. Then he sat down at the table and wrote:

"Glad you got my message, for I think it unsafe to walk out of the castle with that large bundle of securities. Here they are. You will be in Paris, on your motorcycle, in time to catch the morning train to Brussels, where you will hand over the bonds to Z.; and he will negotiate them at once.

"A. L.

"P.S.—As you pass by the Great Oak, tell our chaps that I'm coming. I have some instructions to give them. But everything is going well. No one here has the least suspicion."

He fastened the letter to the parcel and lowered both through the window with a length of string:

"Good," he said. "That's all right. It's a weight off my mind."

He waited a few minutes longer, stalking up and down the room and smiling at the portraits of two gallant gentlemen hanging on the wall:

"Horace de Sarzeau-Vendôme, marshal of France.... And you, the Great Condé... I salute you, my ancestors both. Lupin de Sarzeau-Vendôme will show himself worthy of you."

At last, when the time came, he took his hat and went down. But, when he reached the ground-floor, Angélique burst from her rooms and exclaimed, with a distraught air:

"I say... if you don't mind... I think you had better...."

And then, without saying more, she went in again, leaving a vision of irresponsible terror in her husband's mind.

"She's out of sorts," he said to himself. "Marriage doesn't suit her."

He lit a cigarette and went out, without attaching importance to an incident that ought to have impressed him:

"Poor Angélique! This will all end in a divorce...."

The night outside was dark, with a cloudy sky.

The servants were closing the shutters of the castle. There was no light in the windows, it being the duke's habit to go to bed soon after dinner.

Lupin passed the gatekeeper's lodge and, as he put his foot on the drawbridge, said:

"Leave the gate open. I am going for a breath of air; I shall be back soon."

The patrol-path was on the right and ran along one of the old ramparts, which used to surround the castle with a second and much larger enclosure, until it ended at an almost demolished postern-gate. The park, which skirted a hillock and afterward followed the side of a deep valley, was bordered on the left by thick coppices.

"What a wonderful place for an ambush!" he said. "A regular cutthroat spot!"

He stopped, thinking that he heard a noise. But no, it was a rustling of the leaves. And yet a stone went rattling down the slopes, bounding against the rugged projections of the rock. But, strange to say, nothing seemed to disquiet him. The crisp sea-breeze came blowing over the plains of the headland; and he eagerly filled his lungs with it:

"What a thing it is to be alive!" he thought. "Still young, a member of the old nobility, a multi-millionaire: what could a man want more?"

At a short distance, he saw against the darkness the yet darker outline of the chapel, the ruins of which towered above the path. A few drops of rain began to fall; and he heard a clock strike nine. He quickened his pace. There was a short descent; then the path rose again. And suddenly, he stopped once more.

A hand had seized his.

He drew back, tried to release himself.

But someone stepped from the clump of trees against which he was brushing; and a voice said; "Ssh!... Not a word!..."

He recognized his wife, Angélique:

"What's the matter?" he asked.

She whispered, so low that he could hardly catch the words:

"They are lying in wait for you... they are in there, in the ruins, with their guns...."

"Who?"

"Keep quiet.... Listen...."

They stood for a moment without stirring; then she said:

103

"They are not moving.... Perhaps they never heard me.... Let's go back...."

"But...."

"Come with me."

Her accent was so imperious that he obeyed without further question. But suddenly she took fright:

"Run!... They are coming!... I am sure of it!..."

True enough, they heard a sound of footsteps.

Then, swiftly, still holding him by the hand, she dragged him, with irresistible energy, along a shortcut, following its turns without hesitation in spite of the darkness and the brambles. And they very soon arrived at the drawbridge.

She put her arm in his. The gatekeeper touched his cap. They crossed the courtyard and entered the castle; and she led him to the corner tower in which both of them had their apartments:

"Come in here," she said.

"To your rooms?"

"Yes."

Two maids were sitting up for her. Their mistress ordered them to retire to their bedrooms, on the third floor.

Almost immediately after, there was a knock at the door of the outer room; and a voice called:

"Angélique!"

"Is that you, father?" she asked, suppressing her agitation.

"Yes. Is your husband here?"

"We have just come in."

"Tell him I want to speak to him. Ask him to come to my room. It's important."

"Very well, father, I'll send him to you."

She listened for a few seconds, then returned to the boudoir where her husband was and said:

"I am sure my father is still there."

He moved as though to go out:

"In that case, if he wants to speak to me...."

"My father is not alone," she said, quickly, blocking his way.

"Who is with him?"

"His nephew, Jacques d'Emboise."

There was a moment's silence. He looked at her with a certain astonishment, failing quite to understand his wife's attitude. But, without pausing to go into the matter:

"Ah, so that dear old d'Emboise is there?" he chuckled. "Then the fat's in the fire? Unless, indeed...."

"My father knows everything," she said. "I overheard a conversation between them just now. His nephew has read certain letters.... I hesitated at first about telling you.... Then I thought that my duty...."

He studied her afresh. But, at once conquered by the queerness of the situation, he burst out laughing:

"What? Don't my friends on board ship burn my letters? And they have let their prisoner escape? The idiots! Oh, when you don't see to everything yourself!... No matter, it's distinctly humorous.... D'Emboise versus d'Emboise.... Oh, but suppose I were no longer recognized? Suppose d'Emboise himself were to confuse me with himself?"

He turned to a wash-hand-stand, took a towel, dipped it in the basin and soaped it and, in the twinkling of an eye, wiped the makeup from his face and altered the set of his hair:

"That's it," he said, showing himself to Angélique under the aspect in which she had seen him on the night of the burglary in Paris. "I feel more comfortable like this for a discussion with my father-in-law."

"Where are you going?" she cried, flinging herself in front of the door.

"Why, to join the gentlemen."

"You shall not pass!"

"Why not?"

"Suppose they kill you?"

"Kill me?"

"That's what they mean to do, to kill you... to hide your body somewhere.... Who would know of it?"

"Very well," he said, "from their point of view, they are quite right. But, if I don't go to them, they will come here. That door won't stop them.... Nor you, I'm thinking. Therefore, it's better to have done with it."

"Follow me," commanded Angélique.

She took up the lamp that lit the room, went into her bedroom, pushed aside the wardrobe, which slid easily on hidden castors, pulled back an old tapestry-hanging, and said:

"Here is a door that has not been used for years. My father believes the key to be lost. I have it here. Unlock the door with it. A staircase in the wall will take you to the bottom of the tower. You need only draw the bolts of another door and you will be free."

He could hardly believe his ears. Suddenly, he grasped the meaning of Angélique's whole behaviour. In front of that sad, plain, but wonderfully gentle face, he stood for a moment discountenanced, almost abashed. He no longer thought of laughing. A feeling of respect, mingled with remorse and kindness, overcame him.

"Why are you saving me?" he whispered.

"You are my husband."

He protested:

"No, no... I have stolen that title. The law will never recognize my marriage."

"My father does not want a scandal," she said.

"Just so," he replied, sharply, "just so. I foresaw that; and that was why I had your cousin d'Emboise near at hand. Once I disappear, he becomes your husband. He is the man you have married in the eyes of men."

"You are the man I have married in the eyes of the Church."

"The Church! The Church! There are means of arranging matters with the Church.... Your marriage can be annulled."

"On what pretext that we can admit?"

He remained silent, thinking over all those points which he had not considered, all those points which were trivial and absurd for him, but which were serious for her, and he repeated several times:

"This is terrible… this is terrible…. I should have anticipated…."

And, suddenly, seized with an idea, he clapped his hands and cried:

"There, I have it! I'm hand in glove with one of the chief figures at the Vatican. The Pope never refuses me anything. I shall obtain an audience and I have no doubt that the Holy Father, moved by my entreaties…."

His plan was so humorous and his delight so artless that Angélique could not help smiling; and she said:

"I am your wife in the eyes of God."

She gave him a look that showed neither scorn nor animosity, nor even anger; and he realized that she omitted to see in him the outlaw and the evildoer and remembered only the man who was her husband and to whom the priest had bound her until the hour of death.

He took a step toward her and observed her more attentively. She did not lower her eyes at first. But she blushed. And never had he seen so pathetic a face, marked with such modesty and such dignity. He said to her, as on that first evening in Paris:

"Oh, your eyes… the calm and sadness of your eyes… the beauty of your eyes!"

She dropped her head and stammered:

"Go away… go…"

In the presence of her confusion, he received a quick intuition of the deeper feelings that stirred her, unknown to herself. To that spinster soul, of which he recognized the romantic power of imagination, the unsatisfied yearnings, the poring over old-world books, he suddenly represented, in that exceptional moment and in consequence of the unconventional circumstances of their meetings, somebody special, a Byronic hero, a chivalrous brigand of romance. One evening, in spite of all obstacles, he, the world-famed adventurer, already ennobled in song and story and exalted by his own audacity, had come to her and slipped the magic ring upon her finger: a mystic and passionate betrothal, as in the days of the *Corsair* and *Hernani*…. Greatly moved and touched, he was on the verge of giving way to an enthusiastic impulse and exclaiming:

"Let us go away together!… Let us fly!… You are my bride… my wife…. Share my dangers, my sorrows and my joys…. It will be a strange and vigorous, a proud and magnificent life…."

But Angélique's eyes were raised to his again; and they were so pure and so noble that he blushed in his turn. This was not the woman to whom such words could be addressed.

He whispered:

"Forgive me…. I am a contemptible wretch…. I have wrecked your life…."

"No," she replied, softly. "On the contrary, you have shown me where my real life lies."

He was about to ask her to explain. But she had opened the door and was pointing the way to him. Nothing more could be spoken between them. He went out without a word, bowing very low as he passed.

A month later, Angélique de Sarzeau-Vendôme, Princesse de Bourbon-Condé, lawful wife of Arsène Lupin, took the veil and, under the name of Sister Marie-Auguste, buried herself within the walls of the Visitation Convent.

On the day of the ceremony, the mother superior of the convent received a heavy sealed envelope containing a letter with the following words:

"For Sister Marie-Auguste's poor."

Enclosed with the letter were five hundred banknotes of a thousand francs each.

IX

THE INVISIBLE PRISONER

One day, at about four o'clock, as evening was drawing in, Farmer Goussot, with his four sons, returned from a day's shooting. They were stalwart men, all five of them, long of limb, broad-chested, with faces tanned by sun and wind. And all five displayed, planted on an enormous neck and shoulders, the same small head with the low forehead, thin lips, beaked nose and hard and repellent cast of countenance. They were feared and disliked by all around them. They were a money-grubbing, crafty family; and their word was not to be trusted.

On reaching the old barbican-wall that surrounds the Héberville property, the farmer opened a narrow, massive door, putting the big key back in his pocket after his sons had passed in. And he walked behind them, along the path that led through the orchards. Here and there stood great trees, stripped by the autumn winds, and clumps of pines, the last survivors of the ancient park now covered by old Goussot's farm.

One of the sons said:

"I hope mother has lit a log or two."

"There's smoke coming from the chimney," said the father.

The outhouses and the homestead showed at the end of a lawn; and, above them, the village church, whose steeple seemed to prick the clouds that trailed along the sky.

"All the guns unloaded?" asked old Goussot.

"Mine isn't," said the eldest. "I slipped in a bullet to blow a kestrel's head off...."

He was the one who was proudest of his skill. And he said to his brothers:

"Look at that bough, at the top of the cherry tree. See me snap it off."

On the bough sat a scarecrow, which had been there since spring and which protected the leafless branches with its idiot arms.

He raised his gun and fired.

The figure came tumbling down with large, comic gestures, and was caught on a big, lower branch, where it remained lying stiff on its stomach, with a great top hat on its head of rags and its hay-stuffed legs swaying from right to left above some water that flowed past the cherry tree through a wooden trough.

They all laughed. The father approved:

"A fine shot, my lad. Besides, the old boy was beginning to annoy me. I couldn't take my eyes from my plate at meals without catching sight of that oaf...."

They went a few steps farther. They were not more than thirty yards from the house, when the father stopped suddenly and said:

"Hullo! What's up?"

The sons also had stopped and stood listening. One of them said, under his breath:

"It comes from the house... from the linen-room...."

And another spluttered:

"Sounds like moans.... And mother's alone!"

Suddenly, a frightful scream rang out. All five rushed forward. Another scream, followed by cries of despair.

"We're here! We're coming!" shouted the eldest, who was leading.

And, as it was a roundabout way to the door, he smashed in a window with his fist and sprang into the old people's bedroom. The room next to it was the linen-room, in which Mother Goussot spent most of her time.

"Damnation!" he said, seeing her lying on the floor, with blood all over her face. "Dad! Dad!"

"What? Where is she?" roared old Goussot, appearing on the scene. "Good lord, what's this?... What have they done to your mother?"

She pulled herself together and, with outstretched arm, stammered:

"Run after him!... This way!... This way!... I'm all right... only a scratch or two.... But run, you! He's taken the money."

The father and sons gave a bound:

"He's taken the money!" bellowed old Goussot, rushing to the door to which his wife was pointing. "He's taken the money! Stop thief!"

But a sound of several voices rose at the end of the passage through which the other three sons were coming:

"I saw him! I saw him!"

"So did I! He ran up the stairs."

"No, there he is, he's coming down again!"

A mad steeplechase shook every floor in the house. Farmer Goussot, on reaching the end of the passage, caught sight of a man standing by the front door trying to open it. If he succeeded, it meant safety, escape through the market square and the back lanes of the village.

Interrupted as he was fumbling at the bolts, the man turning stupid, lost his head, charged at old Goussot and sent him spinning, dodged the eldest brother and, pursued by the four sons, doubled back down the long passage, ran into the old couple's bedroom, flung his legs through the broken window and disappeared.

The sons rushed after him across the lawns and orchards, now darkened by the falling night.

"The villain's done for," chuckled old Goussot. "There's no way out for him. The walls are too high. He's done for, the scoundrel!"

The two farmhands returned, at that moment, from the village; and he told them what had happened and gave each of them a gun:

"If the swine shows his nose anywhere near the house," he said, "let fly at him. Give him no mercy!"

He told them where to stand, went to make sure that the farm-gates, which were only used for the carts, were locked, and, not till then, remembered that his wife might perhaps be in need of aid:

"Well, mother, how goes it?"

"Where is he? Have you got him?" she asked, in a breath.

"Yes, we're after him. The lads must have collared him by now."

The news quite restored her; and a nip of rum gave her the strength to drag herself to the bed, with old Goussot's assistance, and to tell her story. For that matter, there was not much to tell. She had just lit the fire in the living-hall; and she was knitting quietly at her bedroom window, waiting for the men to return, when she thought that she heard a slight grating sound in the linen-room next door:

"I must have left the cat in there," she thought to herself.

She went in, suspecting nothing, and was astonished to see the two doors of one of the linen-cupboards, the one in which they hid their money, wide open. She walked up to it, still without suspicion. There was a man there, hiding, with his back to the shelves.

"But how did he get in?" asked old Goussot.

"Through the passage, I suppose. We never keep the back door shut."

"And then did he go for you?"

"No, I went for him. He tried to get away."

"You should have let him."

"And what about the money?"

"Had he taken it by then?"

"Had he taken it! I saw the bundle of banknotes in his hands, the sweep! I would have let him kill me sooner.... Oh, we had a sharp tussle, I give you my word!"

"Then he had no weapon?"

"No more than I did. We had our fingers, our nails and our teeth. Look here, where he bit me. And I yelled and screamed! Only, I'm an old woman you see.... I had to let go of him...."

"Do you know the man?"

"I'm pretty sure it was old Trainard."

"The tramp? Why, of course it's old Trainard!" cried the farmer. "I thought I knew him too.... Besides, he's been hanging round the house these last three days. The old vagabond must have smelt the money. Aha, Trainard, my man, we shall see some fun! A number-one hiding in the first place; and then the police.... I say, mother, you can get up now, can't you? Then go and fetch the neighbours.... Ask them to run for the gendarmes.... By the by, the attorney's youngster has a bicycle.... How that damned old Trainard scooted! He's got good legs for his age, he has. He can run like a hare!"

Goussot was holding his sides, revelling in the occurrence. He risked nothing by waiting. No power on earth could help the tramp escape or keep him from the sound thrashing which he had earned and from being conveyed, under safe escort, to the town gaol.

The farmer took a gun and went out to his two labourers:

"Anything fresh?"

"No, Farmer Goussot, not yet."

"We shan't have long to wait. Unless old Nick carries him over the walls...."

From time to time, they heard the four brothers hailing one another in the distance. The old bird was evidently making a fight for it, was more active than they would have thought. Still, with sturdy fellows like the Goussot brothers....

However, one of them returned, looking rather crestfallen, and made no secret of his opinion:

"It's no use keeping on at it for the present. It's pitch dark. The old chap must have crept into some hole. We'll hunt him out tomorrow."

"Tomorrow! Why, lad, you're off your chump!" protested the farmer.

The eldest son now appeared, quite out of breath, and was of the same opinion as his brother. Why not wait till next day, seeing that the ruffian was as safe within the demesne as between the walls of a prison?

"Well, I'll go myself," cried old Goussot. "Light me a lantern, somebody!"

But, at that moment, three gendarmes arrived; and a number of village lads also came up to hear the latest.

The sergeant of gendarmes was a man of method. He first insisted on hearing the whole story, in full detail; then he stopped to think; then he questioned the four brothers, separately, and took his time for reflection after each deposition. When he had learnt from them that the tramp had fled toward the back of the estate, that he had been lost sight of repeatedly and that he had finally disappeared near a place known as the Crows' Knoll, he meditated once more and announced his conclusion:

"Better wait. Old Trainard might slip through our hands, amidst all the confusion of a pursuit in the dark, and then good night, everybody!"

The farmer shrugged his shoulders and, cursing under his breath, yielded to the sergeant's arguments. That worthy organized a strict watch, distributed the brothers Goussot and the lads from the village under his men's eyes, made sure that the ladders were locked away and established his headquarters in the dining-room, where he and Farmer Goussot sat and nodded over a decanter of old brandy.

The night passed quietly. Every two hours, the sergeant went his rounds and inspected the posts. There were no alarms. Old Trainard did not budge from his hole.

The battle began at break of day.

It lasted four hours.

In those four hours, the thirteen acres of land within the walls were searched, explored, gone over in every direction by a score of men who beat the bushes with sticks, trampled over the tall grass, rummaged in the hollows of the trees and scattered the heaps of dry leaves. And old Trainard remained invisible.

"Well, this is a bit thick!" growled Goussot.

"Beats me altogether," retorted the sergeant.

And indeed there was no explaining the phenomenon. For, after all, apart from a few old clumps of laurels and spindle-trees, which were thoroughly beaten, all the trees were bare. There was no building, no shed, no stack, nothing, in short, that could serve as a hiding-place.

As for the wall, a careful inspection convinced even the sergeant that it was physically impossible to scale it.

In the afternoon, the investigations were begun all over again in the presence of the examining-magistrate and the public-prosecutor's deputy. The results were no more successful. Nay, worse, the officials looked upon the matter as so suspicious that they could not restrain their ill-humour and asked:

"Are you quite sure, Farmer Goussot, that you and your sons haven't been seeing double?"

"And what about my wife?" retorted the farmer, red with anger. "Did she see double when the scamp had her by the throat? Go and look at the marks, if you doubt me!"

"Very well. But then where is the scamp?"

"Here, between those four walls."

"Very well. Then ferret him out. We give it up. It's quite clear, that if a man were hidden within the precincts of this farm, we should have found him by now."

"I swear I'll lay hands on him, true as I stand here!" shouted Farmer Goussot. "It shall not be said that I've been robbed of six thousand francs. Yes, six thousand! There were three cows I sold; and then the wheat-crop; and then the apples. Six thousand-franc notes, which I was just going to take to the bank. Well, I swear to Heaven that the money's as good as in my pocket!"

"That's all right and I wish you luck," said the examining-magistrate, as he went away, followed by the deputy and the gendarmes.

The neighbours also walked off in a more or less facetious mood. And, by the end of the afternoon, none remained but the Goussots and the two farm-labourers.

Old Goussot at once explained his plan. By day, they were to search. At night, they were to keep an incessant watch. It would last as long as it had to. Hang it, old Trainard was a man like other men; and men have to eat and drink! Old Trainard must needs, therefore, come out of his earth to eat and drink.

"At most," said Goussot, "he can have a few crusts of bread in his pocket, or even pull up a root or two at night. But, as far as drink's concerned, no go. There's only the spring. And he'll be a clever dog if he gets near that."

He himself, that evening, took up his stand near the spring. Three hours later, his eldest son relieved him. The other brothers and the farmhands slept in the house, each taking his turn of the watch and keeping all the lamps and candles lit, so that there might be no surprise.

So it went on for fourteen consecutive nights. And for fourteen days, while two of the men and Mother Goussot remained on guard, the five others explored the Héberville ground.

At the end of that fortnight, not a sign.

The farmer never ceased storming. He sent for a retired detective-inspector who lived in the neighbouring town. The inspector stayed with him for a whole week. He found neither old Trainard nor the least clue that could give them any hope of finding old Trainard.

"It's a bit thick!" repeated Farmer Goussot. "For he's there, the rascal! As far as being anywhere goes, he's there. So...."

Planting himself on the threshold, he railed at the enemy at the top of his voice:

"You blithering idiot, would you rather croak in your hole than fork out the money? Then croak, you pig!"

And Mother Goussot, in her turn, yelped, in her shrill voice:

"Is it prison you're afraid of? Hand over the notes and you can hook it!"

But old Trainard did not breathe a word; and the husband and wife tired their lungs in vain.

Shocking days passed. Farmer Goussot could no longer sleep, lay shivering with fever. The sons became morose and quarrelsome and never let their guns out of their hands, having no other idea but to shoot the tramp.

It was the one topic of conversation in the village; and the Goussot story, from being local at first, soon went the round of the press. Newspaper-reporters came from the assize-town, from Paris itself, and were rudely shown the door by Farmer Goussot.

"Each man his own house," he said. "You mind your business. I mind mine. It's nothing to do with anyone."

"Still, Farmer Goussot...."

"Go to blazes!"

And he slammed the door in their face.

Old Trainard had now been hidden within the walls of Héberville for something like four weeks. The Goussots continued their search as doggedly and confidently as ever, but with daily decreasing hope, as though they were confronted with one of those mysterious obstacles which discourage human effort. And the idea that they would never see their money again began to take root in them.

One fine morning, at about ten o'clock, a motorcar, crossing the village square at full speed, broke down and came to a dead stop.

The driver, after a careful inspection, declared that the repairs would take some little time, whereupon the owner of the car resolved to wait at the inn and lunch. He was a gentleman on the right side of forty, with close-cropped side-whiskers and a pleasant expression of face; and he soon made himself at home with the people at the inn.

Of course, they told him the story of the Goussots. He had not heard it before, as he had been abroad; but it seemed to interest him greatly. He made them give him all the details, raised objections, discussed various theories with a number of people who were eating at the same table and ended by exclaiming:

"Nonsense! It can't be so intricate as all that. I have had some experience of this sort of thing. And, if I were on the premises...."

"That's easily arranged," said the innkeeper. "I know Farmer Goussot.... He won't object...."

The request was soon made and granted. Old Goussot was in one of those frames of mind when we are less disposed to protest against outside interference. His wife, at any rate, was very firm:

"Let the gentleman come, if he wants to."

The gentleman paid his bill and instructed his driver to try the car on the highroad as soon as the repairs were finished:

"I shall want an hour," he said, "no more. Be ready in an hour's time."

Then he went to Farmer Goussot's.

He did not say much at the farm. Old Goussot, hoping against hope, was lavish with information, took his visitor along the walls down to the little door opening on the fields, produced the key and gave minute details of all the searches that had been made so far.

Oddly enough, the stranger, who hardly spoke, seemed not to listen either. He merely looked, with a rather vacant gaze. When they had been round the estate, old Goussot asked, anxiously:

"Well?"

"Well what?"

"Do you think you know?"

The visitor stood for a moment without answering. Then he said:

"No, nothing."

"Why, of course not!" cried the farmer, throwing up his arms. "How should you know! It's all hanky-panky. Shall I tell you what I think? Well, that old Trainard has been so jolly clever that he's lying dead in his hole... and the banknotes are rotting with him. Do you hear? You can take my word for it."

The gentleman said, very calmly:

"There's only one thing that interests me. The tramp, all said and done, was free at night and able to feed on what he could pick up. But how about drinking?"

"Out of the question!" shouted the farmer. "Quite out of the question! There's no water except this; and we have kept watch beside it every night."

"It's a spring. Where does it rise?"

"Here, where we stand."

"Is there enough pressure to bring it into the pool of itself?"

"Yes."

"And where does the water go when it runs out of the pool?"

"Into this pipe here, which goes under ground and carries it to the house, for use in the kitchen. So there's no way of drinking, seeing that we were there and that the spring is twenty yards from the house."

"Hasn't it rained during the last four weeks?"

"Not once: I've told you that already."

The stranger went to the spring and examined it. The trough was formed of a few boards of wood joined together just above the ground; and the water ran through it, slow and clear.

"The water's not more than a foot deep, is it?" he asked.

In order to measure it, he picked up from the grass a straw which he dipped into the pool. But, as he was stooping, he suddenly broke off and looked around him.

"Oh, how funny!" he said, bursting into a peal of laughter.

"Why, what's the matter?" spluttered old Goussot, rushing toward the pool, as though a man could have lain hidden between those narrow boards.

And Mother Goussot clasped her hands.

"What is it? Have you seen him? Where is he?"

"Neither in it nor under it," replied the stranger, who was still laughing.

He made for the house, eagerly followed by the farmer, the old woman and the four sons. The innkeeper was there also, as were the people from the inn who had been watching the stranger's movements. And there was a dead silence, while they waited for the extraordinary disclosure.

"It's as I thought," he said, with an amused expression. "The old chap had to quench his thirst somewhere; and, as there was only the spring...."

114

"Oh, but look here," growled Farmer Goussot, "we should have seen him!"

"It was at night."

"We should have heard him... and seen him too, as we were close by."

"So was he."

"And he drank the water from the pool?"

"Yes."

"How?"

"From a little way off."

"With what?"

"With this."

And the stranger showed the straw which he had picked up:

"There, here's the straw for the customer's long drink. You will see, there's more of it than usual: in fact, it is made of three straws stuck into one another. That was the first thing I noticed: those three straws fastened together. The proof is conclusive."

"But, hang it all, the proof of what?" cried Farmer Goussot, irritably.

The stranger took a shotgun from the rack.

"Is it loaded?" he asked.

"Yes," said the youngest of the brothers. "I use it to kill the sparrows with, for fun. It's small shot."

"Capital! A peppering where it won't hurt him will do the trick."

His face suddenly assumed a masterful look. He gripped the farmer by the arm and rapped out, in an imperious tone:

"Listen to me, Farmer Goussot. I'm not here to do policeman's work; and I won't have the poor beggar locked up at any price. Four weeks of starvation and fright is good enough for anybody. So you've got to swear to me, you and your sons, that you'll let him off without hurting him."

"He must hand over the money!"

"Well, of course. Do you swear?"

"I swear."

The gentleman walked back to the doorsill, at the entrance to the orchard. He took a quick aim, pointing his gun a little in the air, in the direction of the cherry tree which overhung the spring. He fired. A hoarse cry rang from the tree; and the scarecrow which had been straddling the main branch for a month past came tumbling to the ground, only to jump up at once and make off as fast as its legs could carry it.

There was a moment's amazement, followed by outcries. The sons darted in pursuit and were not long in coming up with the runaway, hampered as he was by his rags and weakened by privation. But the stranger was already protecting him against their wrath:

"Hands off there! This man belongs to me. I won't have him touched.... I hope I haven't stung you up too much, Trainard?"

Standing on his straw legs wrapped round with strips of tattered cloth, with his arms and his whole body clad in the same materials, his head swathed in linen, tightly packed like a sausage, the old chap still had the stiff appearance of a lay-figure. And the whole effect was so ludicrous and so unexpected that the onlookers screamed with laughter.

The stranger unbound his head; and they saw a veiled mask of tangled grey beard encroaching on every side upon a skeleton face lit up by two eyes burning with fever.

The laughter was louder than ever.

"The money! The six notes!" roared the farmer.

The stranger kept him at a distance:

"One moment... we'll give you that back, shan't we, Trainard?"

And, taking his knife and cutting away the straw and cloth, he jested, cheerily:

"You poor old beggar, what a guy you look! But how on earth did you manage to pull off that trick? You must be confoundedly clever, or else you had the devil's own luck.... So, on the first night, you used the breathing-time they left you to rig yourself in these togs! Not a bad idea. Who could ever suspect a scarecrow?... They were so accustomed to seeing it stuck up in its tree! But, poor old daddy, how uncomfortable you must have felt, lying flat up there on your stomach, with your arms and legs dangling down! All day long, like that! The deuce of an attitude! And how you must have been put to it, when you ventured to move a limb, eh? And how you must have funked going to sleep!... And then you had to eat! And drink! And you heard the sentry and felt the barrel of his gun within a yard of your nose! *Brrrr!*... But the trickiest of all, you know, was your bit of straw!... Upon my word, when I think that, without a sound, without a movement so to speak, you had to fish out lengths of straw from your toggery, fix them end to end, let your apparatus down to the water and suck up the heavenly moisture drop by drop.... Upon my word, one could scream with admiration.... Well done, Trainard...." And he added, between his teeth, "Only you're in a very unappetizing state, my man. Haven't you washed yourself all this month, you old pig? After all, you had as much water as you wanted!... Here, you people, I hand him over to you. I'm going to wash my hands, that's what I'm going to do."

Farmer Goussot and his four sons grabbed at the prey which he was abandoning to them:

"Now then, come along, fork out the money."

Dazed as he was, the tramp still managed to simulate astonishment.

"Don't put on that idiot look," growled the farmer. "Come on. Out with the six notes...."

"What?... What do you want of me?" stammered old Trainard.

"The money... on the nail...."

"What money?"

"The banknotes."

"The banknotes?"

"Oh, I'm getting sick of you! Here, lads...."

They laid the old fellow flat, tore off the rags that composed his clothes, felt and searched him all over.

There was nothing on him.

"You thief and you robber!" yelled old Goussot. "What have you done with it?"

The old beggar seemed more dazed than ever. Too cunning to confess, he kept on whining:

"What do you want of me?... Money? I haven't three sous to call my own...."

But his eyes, wide with wonder, remained fixed upon his clothes; and he himself seemed not to understand.

The Goussots' rage could no longer be restrained. They rained blows upon him, which did not improve matters. But the farmer was convinced that Trainard had hidden the money before turning himself into the scarecrow:

"Where have you put it, you scum? Out with it! In what part of the orchard have you hidden it?"

"The money?" repeated the tramp with a stupid look.

"Yes, the money! The money which you've buried somewhere.... Oh, if we don't find it, your goose is cooked!... We have witnesses, haven't we?... All of you, friends, eh? And then the gentleman...."

He turned, with the intention of addressing the stranger, in the direction of the spring, which was thirty or forty steps to the left. And he was quite surprised not to see him washing his hands there:

"Has he gone?" he asked.

Someone answered:

"No, he lit a cigarette and went for a stroll in the orchard."

"Oh, that's all right!" said the farmer. "He's the sort to find the notes for us, just as he found the man."

"Unless..." said a voice.

"Unless what?" echoed the farmer. "What do you mean? Have you something in your head? Out with it, then! What is it?"

But he interrupted himself suddenly, seized with a doubt; and there was a moment's silence. The same idea dawned on all the country-folk. The stranger's arrival at Héberville, the breakdown of his motor, his manner of questioning the people at the inn and of gaining admission to the farm: were not all these part and parcel of a put-up job, the trick of a cracksman who had learnt the story from the papers and who had come to try his luck on the spot?...

"Jolly smart of him!" said the innkeeper. "He must have taken the money from old Trainard's pocket, before our eyes, while he was searching him."

"Impossible!" spluttered Farmer Goussot. "He would have been seen going out that way... by the house... whereas he's strolling in the orchard."

Mother Goussot, all of a heap, suggested:

"The little door at the end, down there?..."

"The key never leaves me."

"But you showed it to him."

"Yes; and I took it back again.... Look, here it is."

He clapped his hand to his pocket and uttered a cry:

"Oh, dash it all, it's gone!... He's sneaked it!..."

He at once rushed away, followed and escorted by his sons and a number of the villagers.

When they were halfway down the orchard, they heard the throb of a motorcar, obviously the one belonging to the stranger, who had given orders to his chauffeur to wait for him at that lower entrance.

When the Goussots reached the door, they saw scrawled with a brick, on the worm-eaten panel, the two words:

"ARSÈNE LUPIN."

117

Stick to it as the angry Goussots might, they found it impossible to prove that old Trainard had stolen any money. Twenty persons had to bear witness that, when all was said, nothing was discovered on his person. He escaped with a few months' imprisonment for the assault.

He did not regret them. As soon as he was released, he was secretly informed that, every quarter, on a given date, at a given hour, under a given milestone on a given road, he would find three gold louis.

To a man like old Trainard that means wealth.

X

Edith Swan-Neck

"Arsène Lupin, what's your real opinion of Inspector Ganimard?"

"A very high one, my dear fellow."

"A very high one? Then why do you never miss a chance of turning him into ridicule?"

"It's a bad habit; and I'm sorry for it. But what can I say? It's the way of the world. Here's a decent detective-chap, here's a whole pack of decent men, who stand for law and order, who protect us against the apaches, who risk their lives for honest people like you and me; and we have nothing to give them in return but flouts and gibes. It's preposterous!"

"Bravo, Lupin! you're talking like a respectable ratepayer!"

"What else am I? I may have peculiar views about other people's property; but I assure you that it's very different when my own's at stake. By Jove, it doesn't do to lay hands on what belongs to me! Then I'm out for blood! Aha! It's *my* pocket, *my* money, *my* watch... hands off! I have the soul of a conservative, my dear fellow, the instincts of a retired tradesman and a due respect for every sort of tradition and authority. And that is why Ganimard inspires me with no little gratitude and esteem."

"But not much admiration?"

"Plenty of admiration too. Over and above the dauntless courage which comes natural to all those gentry at the Criminal Investigation Department, Ganimard possesses very sterling qualities: decision, insight and judgment. I have watched him at work. He's somebody, when all's said. Do you know the Edith Swan-neck story, as it was called?"

"I know as much as everybody knows."

"That means that you don't know it at all. Well, that job was, I daresay, the one which I thought out most cleverly, with the utmost care and the utmost precaution, the one which I shrouded in the greatest darkness and mystery, the one which it took the biggest generalship to carry through. It was a regular game of chess, played according to strict scientific and mathematical rules. And yet Ganimard ended by unravelling the knot. Thanks to him, they know the truth today on the Quai des Orfèvres. And it is a truth quite out of the common, I assure you."

"May I hope to hear it?"

"Certainly... one of these days... when I have time.... But the Brunelli is dancing at the Opera tonight; and, if she were not to see me in my stall...!"

I do not meet Lupin often. He confesses with difficulty, when it suits him. It was only gradually, by snatches, by odds and ends of confidences, that I was able to obtain the different incidents and to piece the story together in all its details.

The main features are well known and I will merely mention the facts.

Three years ago, when the train from Brest arrived at Rennes, the door of one of the luggage vans was found smashed in. This van had been booked by Colonel Sparmiento, a rich Brazilian, who was travelling with his wife in the same train. It contained a complete set of tapestry-hangings. The case in which one of these was packed had been broken open and the tapestry had disappeared.

Colonel Sparmiento started proceedings against the railway-company, claiming heavy damages, not only for the stolen tapestry, but also for the loss in value which the whole collection suffered in consequence of the theft.

The police instituted inquiries. The company offered a large reward. A fortnight later, a letter which had come undone in the post was opened by the authorities and revealed the fact that the theft had been carried out under the direction of Arsène Lupin and that a package was to leave next day for the United States. That same evening, the tapestry was discovered in a trunk deposited in the cloakroom at the Gare Saint-Lazare.

The scheme, therefore, had miscarried. Lupin felt the disappointment so much that he vented his ill-humour in a communication to Colonel Sparmiento, ending with the following words, which were clear enough for anybody:

"It was very considerate of me to take only one. Next time, I shall take the twelve. *Verbum sap.*

"A. L."

Colonel Sparmiento had been living for some months in a house standing at the end of a small garden at the corner of the Rue de la Faisanderie and the Rue Dufresnoy. He was a rather thickset, broad-shouldered man, with black hair and a swarthy skin, always well and quietly dressed. He was married to an extremely pretty but delicate Englishwoman, who was much upset by the business of the tapestries. From the first she implored her husband to sell them for what they would fetch. The Colonel had much too forcible and dogged a nature to yield to what he had every right to describe as a woman's fancies. He sold nothing, but he redoubled his precautions and adopted every measure that was likely to make an attempt at burglary impossible.

To begin with, so that he might confine his watch to the garden-front, he walled up all the windows on the ground-floor and the first floor overlooking the Rue Dufresnoy. Next, he enlisted the services of a firm which made a speciality of protecting private houses against robberies. Every window of the gallery in which the tapestries were hung was fitted with invisible burglar alarms, the position of which was known, to none but himself. These, at the least touch, switched on all the electric lights and set a whole system of bells and gongs ringing.

In addition to this, the insurance companies to which he applied refused to grant policies to any considerable amount unless he consented to let three men, supplied by the companies and paid by himself, occupy the ground-floor of his house every night. They selected for the purpose three ex-detectives, tried and trustworthy men, all of whom hated Lupin like poison. As for the servants, the colonel had known them for years and was ready to vouch for them.

After taking these steps and organizing the defence of the house as though it were a fortress, the colonel gave a great housewarming, a sort of private view, to which he invited the members of both his clubs, as well as a certain number of ladies, journalists, art-patrons and critics.

They felt, as they passed through the garden-gate, much as if they were walking into a prison. The three private detectives, posted at the foot of the stairs, asked for each visitor's invitation card and eyed him up and down suspiciously, making him feel as though they were going to search his pockets or take his fingerprints.

The colonel, who received his guests on the first floor, made laughing apologies and seemed delighted at the opportunity of explaining the arrangements which he had invented to secure the safety of his hangings. His wife stood by him, looking charmingly young and pretty, fair-haired, pale and sinuous, with a sad and gentle expression, the expression of resignation often worn by those who are threatened by fate.

When all the guests had come, the garden-gates and the hall-doors were closed. Then everybody filed into the middle gallery, which was reached through two steel doors, while its windows, with their huge shutters, were protected by iron bars. This was where the twelve tapestries were kept.

They were matchless works of art and, taking their inspiration from the famous Bayeux Tapestry, attributed to Queen Matilda, they represented the story of the Norman Conquest. They had been ordered in the fourteenth century by the descendant of a man-at-arms in William the Conqueror's train; were executed by Jehan Gosset, a famous Arras weaver; and were discovered, five hundred years later, in an old Breton manor-house. On hearing of this, the colonel had struck a bargain for fifty thousand francs. They were worth ten times the money.

But the finest of the twelve hangings composing the set, the most uncommon because the subject had not been treated by Queen Matilda, was the one which Arsène Lupin had stolen and which had been so fortunately recovered. It portrayed Edith Swan-neck on the battlefield of Hastings, seeking among the dead for the body of her sweetheart Harold, last of the Saxon kings.

The guests were lost in enthusiasm over this tapestry, over the unsophisticated beauty of the design, over the faded colours, over the lifelike grouping of the figures and the pitiful sadness of the scene. Poor Edith Swan-neck stood drooping like an overweighted lily. Her white gown revealed the lines of her languid figure. Her long, tapering hands were outstretched in a gesture of terror and entreaty. And nothing could be more mournful than her profile, over which flickered the most dejected and despairing of smiles.

"A harrowing smile," remarked one of the critics, to whom the others listened with deference. "A very charming smile, besides; and it reminds me, Colonel, of the smile of Mme. Sparmiento."

And seeing that the observation seemed to meet with approval, he enlarged upon his idea:

"There are other points of resemblance that struck me at once, such as the very graceful curve of the neck and the delicacy of the hands... and also something about the figure, about the general attitude...."

"What you say is so true," said the colonel, "that I confess that it was this likeness that decided me to buy the hangings. And there was another reason, which was that, by a really curious chance, my wife's name happens to be Edith. I have called her Edith Swan-neck ever since." And the colonel added, with a laugh, "I hope that the coincidence will stop at this and that my dear Edith will never have to go in search of her true-love's body, like her prototype."

He laughed as he uttered these words, but his laugh met with no echo; and we find the same impression of awkward silence in all the accounts of the evening that appeared during the next few days. The people standing near him did not know what to say. One of them tried to jest:

"Your name isn't Harold, Colonel?"

"No, thank you," he declared, with continued merriment. "No, that's not my name; nor am I in the least like the Saxon king."

All have since agreed in stating that, at that moment, as the colonel finished speaking, the first alarm rang from the windows—the right or the middle window: opinions differ on this point—rang short and shrill on a single note. The peal of the alarm-bell was followed by an exclamation of terror uttered by Mme. Sparmiento, who caught hold of her husband's arm. He cried:

"What's the matter? What does this mean?"

The guests stood motionless, with their eyes staring at the windows. The colonel repeated:

"What does it mean? I don't understand. No one but myself knows where that bell is fixed...."

And, at that moment—here again the evidence is unanimous—at that moment came sudden, absolute darkness, followed immediately by the maddening din of all the bells and all the gongs, from top to bottom of the house, in every room and at every window.

For a few seconds, a stupid disorder, an insane terror, reigned. The women screamed. The men banged with their fists on the closed doors. They hustled and fought. People fell to the floor and were trampled under foot. It was like a panic-stricken crowd, scared by threatening flames or by a bursting shell. And, above the uproar, rose the colonel's voice, shouting:

"Silence!... Don't move!... It's all right!... The switch is over there, in the corner.... Wait a bit.... Here!"

He had pushed his way through his guests and reached a corner of the gallery; and, all at once, the electric light blazed up again, while the pandemonium of bells stopped.

Then, in the sudden light, a strange sight met the eyes. Two ladies had fainted. Mme. Sparmiento, hanging to her husband's arm, with her knees dragging on the floor, and livid in the face, appeared half dead. The men, pale, with their neckties awry, looked as if they had all been in the wars.

"The tapestries are there!" cried someone.

There was a great surprise, as though the disappearance of those hangings ought to have been the natural result and the only plausible explanation of the incident. But nothing had been moved. A few valuable pictures, hanging on the walls, were there still. And, though the same din had reverberated all over the house, though all the rooms had been thrown into darkness, the detectives had seen no one entering or trying to enter.

"Besides," said the colonel, "it's only the windows of the gallery that have alarms. Nobody but myself understands how they work; and I had not set them yet."

People laughed loudly at the way in which they had been frightened, but they laughed without conviction and in a more or less shamefaced fashion, for each of them was keenly alive to the absurdity of his conduct. And they had but one thought—to get out of that house where, say what you would, the atmosphere was one of agonizing anxiety.

Two journalists stayed behind, however; and the colonel joined them, after attending to Edith and handing her over to her maids. The three of them, together with the detectives, made a search that did not lead to the discovery of anything of the least interest. Then the colonel sent for some champagne; and the result was that it was not until a late hour—to be exact, a quarter to three in the morning—that the journalists took their leave, the colonel retired to his quarters, and the detectives withdrew to the room which had been set aside for them on the ground-floor.

They took the watch by turns, a watch consisting, in the first place, in keeping awake and, next, in looking round the garden and visiting the gallery at intervals.

These orders were scrupulously carried out, except between five and seven in the morning, when sleep gained the mastery and the men ceased to go their rounds. But it was broad daylight out of doors. Besides, if there had been the least sound of bells, would they not have woke up?

Nevertheless, when one of them, at twenty minutes past seven, opened the door of the gallery and flung back the shutters, he saw that the twelve tapestries were gone.

This man and the others were blamed afterward for not giving the alarm at once and for starting their own investigations before informing the colonel and telephoning to the local commissary. Yet this very excusable delay can hardly be said to have hampered the action of the police. In any case, the colonel was not told until half-past eight. He was dressed and ready to go out. The news did not seem to upset him beyond measure, or, at least, he managed to control his emotion. But the effort must have been too much for him, for he suddenly dropped into a chair and, for some moments, gave way to a regular fit of despair and anguish, most painful to behold in a man of his resolute appearance.

Recovering and mastering himself, he went to the gallery, stared at the bare walls and then sat down at a table and hastily scribbled a letter, which he put into an envelope and sealed.

"There," he said. "I'm in a hurry.... I have an important engagement.... Here is a letter for the commissary of police." And, seeing the detectives' eyes upon him, he added, "I am giving the commissary my views... telling him of a suspicion that occurs to me.... He must follow it up.... I will do what I can...."

He left the house at a run, with excited gestures which the detectives were subsequently to remember.

A few minutes later, the commissary of police arrived. He was handed the letter, which contained the following words:

"I am at the end of my tether. The theft of those tapestries completes the crash which I have been trying to conceal for the past year. I bought them as a speculation and was hoping to get a million francs for them, thanks to the fuss that was made about them. As it was, an American offered me six hundred thousand. It meant my salvation. This means utter destruction.

"I hope that my dear wife will forgive the sorrow which I am bringing upon her. Her name will be on my lips at the last moment."

Mme. Sparmiento was informed. She remained aghast with horror, while inquiries were instituted and attempts made to trace the colonel's movements.

Late in the afternoon, a telephone-message came from Ville d'Avray. A gang of railwaymen had found a man's body lying at the entrance to a tunnel after a train had passed. The body was hideously mutilated; the face had lost all resemblance to anything human. There were no papers in the pockets. But the description answered to that of the colonel.

Mme. Sparmiento arrived at Ville d'Avray, by motorcar, at seven o'clock in the evening. She was taken to a room at the railway-station. When the sheet that covered it was removed, Edith, Edith Swan-neck, recognized her husband's body.

In these circumstances, Lupin did not receive his usual good notices in the press: "Let him look to himself," jeered one leader-writer, summing up the general opinion. "It would not take many exploits of this kind for him to forfeit the popularity which has not been grudged him hitherto. We have no use for Lupin, except when his rogueries are perpetrated at the expense of shady company-promoters, foreign adventurers, German barons, banks and financial companies. And, above all, no murders! A burglar we can put up with; but a murderer, no! If he is not directly guilty, he is at least responsible for this death. There is blood upon his hands; the arms on his escutcheon are stained gules...."

The public anger and disgust were increased by the pity which Edith's pale face aroused. The guests of the night before gave their version of what had happened, omitting none of the impressive details; and a legend formed straightway around the fair-haired Englishwoman, a legend that assumed a really tragic character, owing to the popular story of the swan-necked heroine.

And yet the public could not withhold its admiration of the extraordinary skill with which the theft had been effected. The police explained it, after a fashion. The detectives had noticed from the first and subsequently stated that one of the three windows of the gallery was wide open. There could be no doubt that Lupin and his confederates had entered through this window. It seemed a very plausible suggestion. Still, in that case, how were they able, first, to climb the garden railings, in coming and going, without being seen; secondly, to cross the garden and put up a ladder on the flower-border, without leaving the least trace behind; thirdly, to open the shutters and the window, without starting the bells and switching on the lights in the house?

The police accused the three detectives of complicity. The magistrate in charge of the case examined them at length, made minute inquiries into their private lives and stated formally that they were above all suspicion. As for the tapestries, there seemed to be no hope that they would be recovered.

It was at this moment that Chief-inspector Ganimard returned from India, where he had been hunting for Lupin on the strength of a number of most convincing proofs supplied by former confederates of Lupin himself. Feeling that he had once more been tricked by his everlasting adversary, fully believing that Lupin had dispatched him on this wild-goose chase so as to be rid of him during the business of the tapestries, he asked for a fortnight's leave of absence, called on Mme. Sparmiento and promised to avenge her husband.

Edith had reached the point at which not even the thought of vengeance relieves the sufferer's pain. She had dismissed the three detectives on the day of the funeral and engaged just one man and an old cook-housekeeper to take the place of the large staff of servants the sight of whom reminded her too cruelly of the past. Not caring what happened, she kept her room and left Ganimard free to act as he pleased.

He took up his quarters on the ground-floor and at once instituted a series of the most minute investigations. He started the inquiry afresh, questioned the people in the neighbourhood, studied the distribution of the rooms and set each of the burglar-alarms going thirty and forty times over.

At the end of the fortnight, he asked for an extension of leave. The chief of the detective-service, who was at that time M. Dudouis, came to see him and found him perched on the top of a ladder, in the gallery. That day, the chief-inspector admitted that all his searches had proved useless.

Two days later, however, M. Dudouis called again and discovered Ganimard in a very thoughtful frame of mind. A bundle of newspapers lay spread in front of him. At last, in reply to his superior's urgent questions, the chief-inspector muttered:

"I know nothing, chief, absolutely nothing; but there's a confounded notion worrying me.... Only it seems so absurd.... And then it doesn't explain things.... On the contrary, it confuses them rather...."

"Then...?"

"Then I implore you, chief, to have a little patience... to let me go my own way. But if I telephone to you, some day or other, suddenly, you must jump into a taxi, without losing a minute. It will mean that I have discovered the secret."

Forty-eight hours passed. Then, one morning, M. Dudouis received a telegram:
"Going to Lille.

"GANIMARD."

"What the dickens can he want to go to Lille for?" wondered the chief-detective.

The day passed without news, followed by another day. But M. Dudouis had every confidence in Ganimard. He knew his man, knew that the old detective was not one of those people who excite themselves for nothing. When Ganimard "got a move on him," it meant that he had sound reasons for doing so.

As a matter of fact, on the evening of that second day, M. Dudouis was called to the telephone.

"Is that you, chief?"

"Is it Ganimard speaking?"

Cautious men both, they began by making sure of each other's identity. As soon as his mind was eased on this point, Ganimard continued, hurriedly:

"Ten men, chief, at once. And please come yourself."

"Where are you?"

"In the house, on the ground-floor. But I will wait for you just inside the garden-gate."

"I'll come at once. In a taxi, of course?"

"Yes, chief. Stop the taxi fifty yards from the house. I'll let you in when you whistle."

Things took place as Ganimard had arranged. Shortly after midnight, when all the lights were out on the upper floors, he slipped into the street and went to meet M. Dudouis. There was a hurried consultation. The officers distributed themselves as Ganimard ordered. Then the chief and the chief-inspector walked back together, noiselessly crossed the garden and closeted themselves with every precaution:

"Well, what's it all about?" asked M. Dudouis. "What does all this mean? Upon my word, we look like a pair of conspirators!"

But Ganimard was not laughing. His chief had never seen him in such a state of perturbation, nor heard him speak in a voice denoting such excitement:

"Any news, Ganimard?"

"Yes, chief, and… this time…! But I can hardly believe it myself…. And yet I'm not mistaken: I know the real truth…. It may be as unlikely as you please, but it is the truth, the whole truth and nothing but the truth."

He wiped away the drops of perspiration that trickled down his forehead and, after a further question from M. Dudouis, pulled himself together, swallowed a glass of water and began:

"Lupin has often got the better of me…."

"Look here, Ganimard," said M. Dudouis, interrupting him. "Why can't you come straight to the point? Tell me, in two words, what's happened."

"No, chief," retorted the chief-inspector, "it is essential that you should know the different stages which I have passed through. Excuse me, but I consider it indispensable." And he repeated: "I was saying, chief, that Lupin has often got the better of me and led me many a dance. But, in this contest in which I have always come out worst… so far… I have at least gained experience of his manner of play and learnt to know his tactics. Now, in the matter of the tapestries, it occurred to me almost from the start to set myself two problems. In the first place, Lupin, who never makes a move without knowing what he is after, was obviously aware that Colonel Sparmiento had come to the end of his money and that the loss of the tapestries might drive him to suicide. Nevertheless, Lupin, who hates the very thought of bloodshed, stole the tapestries."

"There was the inducement," said M. Dudouis, "of the five or six hundred thousand francs which they are worth."

"No, chief, I tell you once more, whatever the occasion might be, Lupin would not take life, nor be the cause of another person's death, for anything in this world, for millions and millions. That's the first point. In the second place, what was the object of all that disturbance, in the evening, during the housewarming party? Obviously, don't you think, to surround the business with an atmosphere of anxiety and terror, in the shortest possible time, and also to divert suspicion from the truth, which, otherwise, might easily have been suspected?… You seem not to understand, chief?"

"Upon my word, I do not!"

"As a matter of fact," said Ganimard, "as a matter of fact, it is not particularly plain. And I myself, when I put the problem before my mind in those same words, did not understand it very clearly…. And yet I felt that I was on the right track…. Yes, there was no doubt about it that Lupin wanted to divert suspicions… to divert them to himself, Lupin, mark you… so that the real person who was working the business might remain unknown…."

"A confederate," suggested M. Dudouis. "A confederate, moving among the visitors, who set the alarms going... and who managed to hide in the house after the party had broken up."

"You're getting warm, chief, you're getting warm! It is certain that the tapestries, as they cannot have been stolen by anyone making his way surreptitiously into the house, were stolen by somebody who remained in the house; and it is equally certain that, by taking the list of the people invited and inquiring into the antecedents of each of them, one might...."

"Well?"

"Well, chief, there's a 'but,' namely, that the three detectives had this list in their hands when the guests arrived and that they still had it when the guests left. Now sixty-three came in and sixty-three went away. So you see...."

"Then do you suppose a servant?..."

"No."

"The detectives?"

"No."

"But, still... but, still," said the chief, impatiently, "if the robbery was committed from the inside...."

"That is beyond dispute," declared the inspector, whose excitement seemed to be nearing fever-point. "There is no question about it. All my investigations led to the same certainty. And my conviction gradually became so positive that I ended, one day, by drawing up this startling axiom: in theory and in fact, the robbery can only have been committed with the assistance of an accomplice staying in the house. Whereas there was no accomplice!"

"That's absurd," said Dudouis.

"Quite absurd," said Ganimard. "But, at the very moment when I uttered that absurd sentence, the truth flashed upon me."

"Eh?"

"Oh, a very dim, very incomplete, but still sufficient truth! With that clue to guide me, I was bound to find the way. Do you follow me, chief?"

M. Dudouis sat silent. The same phenomenon that had taken place in Ganimard was evidently taking place in him. He muttered:

"If it's not one of the guests, nor the servants, nor the private detectives, then there's no one left...."

"Yes, chief, there's one left...."

M. Dudouis started as though he had received a shock; and, in a voice that betrayed his excitement:

"But, look here, that's preposterous."

"Why?"

"Come, think for yourself!"

"Go on, chief: say what's in your mind."

"Nonsense! What do you mean?"

"Go on, chief."

"It's impossible! How can Sparmiento have been Lupin's accomplice?"

Ganimard gave a little chuckle.

"Exactly, Arsène Lupin's accomplice!... That explains everything. During the night, while the three detectives were downstairs watching, or sleeping rather, for Colonel Sparmiento had given them champagne to drink and perhaps doctored it beforehand, the said colonel took down the hangings and passed them out through the window of his bedroom. The room is on the second floor and looks out on another street, which was not watched, because the lower windows are walled up."

M. Dudouis reflected and then shrugged his shoulders:

"It's preposterous!" he repeated.

"Why?"

"Why? Because, if the colonel had been Arsène Lupin's accomplice, he would not have committed suicide after achieving his success."

"Who says that he committed suicide?"

"Why, he was found dead on the line!"

"I told you, there is no such thing as death with Lupin."

"Still, this was genuine enough. Besides, Mme. Sparmiento identified the body."

"I thought you would say that, chief. The argument worried me too. There was I, all of a sudden, with three people in front of me instead of one: first, Arsène Lupin, cracksman; secondly, Colonel Sparmiento, his accomplice; thirdly, a dead man. Spare us! It was too much of a good thing!"

Ganimard took a bundle of newspapers, untied it and handed one of them to Mr. Dudouis:

"You remember, chief, last time you were here, I was looking through the papers.... I wanted to see if something had not happened, at that period, that might bear upon the case and confirm my supposition. Please read this paragraph."

M. Dudouis took the paper and read aloud:

"Our Lille correspondent informs us that a curious incident has occurred in that town. A corpse has disappeared from the local morgue, the corpse of a man unknown who threw himself under the wheels of a steam tramcar on the day before. No one is able to suggest a reason for this disappearance."

M. Dudouis sat thinking and then asked:

"So... you believe...?"

"I have just come from Lille," replied Ganimard, "and my inquiries leave not a doubt in my mind. The corpse was removed on the same night on which Colonel Sparmiento gave his housewarming. It was taken straight to Ville d'Avray by motorcar; and the car remained near the railway-line until the evening."

"Near the tunnel, therefore," said M. Dudouis.

"Next to it, chief."

"So that the body which was found is merely that body, dressed in Colonel Sparmiento's clothes."

"Precisely, chief."

"Then Colonel Sparmiento is not dead?"

"No more dead than you or I, chief."

"But then why all these complications? Why the theft of one tapestry, followed by its recovery, followed by the theft of the twelve? Why that housewarming? Why that disturbance? Why everything? Your story won't hold water, Ganimard."

"Only because you, chief, like myself, have stopped halfway; because, strange as this story already sounds, we must go still farther, very much farther, in the direction of the improbable and the astounding. And why not, after all? Remember that we are dealing with Arsène Lupin. With him, is it not always just the improbable and the astounding that we must look for? Must we not always go straight for the maddest suppositions? And, when I say the maddest, I am using the wrong word. On the contrary, the whole thing is wonderfully logical and so simple that a child could understand it. Confederates only betray you. Why employ confederates, when it is so easy and so natural to act for yourself, by yourself, with your own hands and by the means within your own reach?"

"What are you saying?... What are you saying?... What are you saying?" cried M. Dudouis, in a sort of singsong voice and a tone of bewilderment that increased with each separate exclamation.

Ganimard gave a fresh chuckle.

"Takes your breath away, chief, doesn't it? So it did mine, on the day when you came to see me here and when the notion was beginning to grow upon me. I was flabbergasted with astonishment. And yet I've had experience of my customer. I know what he's capable of.... But this, no, this was really a bit too stiff!"

"It's impossible! It's impossible!" said M. Dudouis, in a low voice.

"On the contrary, chief, it's quite possible and quite logical and quite normal. It's the threefold incarnation of one and the same individual. A schoolboy would solve the problem in a minute, by a simple process of elimination. Take away the dead man: there remains Sparmiento and Lupin. Take away Sparmiento...."

"There remains Lupin," muttered the chief-detective.

"Yes, chief, Lupin simply, Lupin in five letters and two syllables, Lupin taken out of his Brazilian skin, Lupin revived from the dead, Lupin translated, for the past six months, into Colonel Sparmiento, travelling in Brittany, hearing of the discovery of the twelve tapestries, buying them, planning the theft of the best of them, so as to draw attention to himself, Lupin, and divert it from himself, Sparmiento. Next, he brings about, in full view of the gaping public, a noisy contest between Lupin and Sparmiento or Sparmiento and Lupin, plots and gives the housewarming party, terrifies his guests and, when everything is ready, arranges for Lupin to steal Sparmiento's tapestries and for Sparmiento, Lupin's victim, to disappear from sight and die unsuspected, unsuspectable, regretted by his friends, pitied by the public and leaving behind him, to pocket the profits of the swindle...."

Ganimard stopped, looked the chief in the eyes and, in a voice that emphasized the importance of his words, concluded:

"Leaving behind him a disconsolate widow."

"Mme. Sparmiento! You really believe....?

"Hang it all!" said the chief-inspector. "People don't work up a whole business of this sort, without seeing something ahead of them... solid profits."

"But the profits, it seems to me, lie in the sale of the tapestries which Lupin will effect in America or elsewhere."

"First of all, yes. But Colonel Sparmiento could effect that sale just as well. And even better. So there's something more."

"Something more?"

"Come, chief, you're forgetting that Colonel Sparmiento has been the victim of an important robbery and that, though he may be dead, at least his widow remains. So it's his widow who will get the money."

"What money?"

"What money? Why, the money due to her! The insurance-money, of course!"

M. Dudouis was staggered. The whole business suddenly became clear to him, with its real meaning. He muttered:

"That's true!... That's true!... The colonel had insured his tapestries...."

"Rather! And for no trifle either."

"For how much?"

"Eight hundred thousand francs."

"Eight hundred thousand?"

"Just so. In five different companies."

"And has Mme. Sparmiento had the money?"

"She got a hundred and fifty thousand francs yesterday and two hundred thousand today, while I was away. The remaining payments are to be made in the course of this week."

"But this is terrible! You ought to have...."

"What, chief? To begin with, they took advantage of my absence to settle up accounts with the companies. I only heard about it on my return when I ran up against an insurance-manager whom I happen to know and took the opportunity of drawing him out."

The chief-detective was silent for some time, not knowing what to say. Then he mumbled:

"What a fellow, though!"

Ganimard nodded his head:

"Yes, chief, a blackguard, but, I can't help saying, a devil of a clever fellow. For his plan to succeed, he must have managed in such a way that, for four or five weeks, no one could express or even conceive the least suspicion of the part played by Colonel Sparmiento. All the indignation and all the inquiries had to be concentrated upon Lupin alone. In the last resort, people had to find themselves faced simply with a mournful, pitiful, penniless widow, poor Edith Swan-neck, a beautiful and legendary vision, a creature so pathetic that the gentlemen of the insurance-companies were almost glad to place something in her hands to relieve her poverty and her grief. That's what was wanted and that's what happened."

The two men were close together and did not take their eyes from each other's faces. The chief asked:

"Who is that woman?"

"Sonia Kritchnoff."

"Sonia Kritchnoff?"

"Yes, the Russian girl whom I arrested last year at the time of the theft of the coronet, and whom Lupin helped to escape."

"Are you sure?"

"Absolutely. I was put off the scent, like everybody else, by Lupin's machinations, and had paid no particular attention to her. But, when I knew the part which she was playing,

I remembered. She is certainly Sonia, metamorphosed into an Englishwoman; Sonia, the most innocent-looking and the trickiest of actresses; Sonia, who would not hesitate to face death for love of Lupin."

"A good capture, Ganimard," said M. Dudouis, approvingly.

"I've something better still for you, chief!"

"Really? What?"

"Lupin's old foster-mother."

"Victoire?"

"She has been here since Mme. Sparmiento began playing the widow; she's the cook."

"Oho!" said M. Dudouis. "My congratulations, Ganimard!"

"I've something for you, chief, that's even better than that!"

M. Dudouis gave a start. The inspector's hand clutched his and was shaking with excitement.

"What do you mean, Ganimard?"

"Do you think, chief, that I would have brought you here, at this late hour, if I had had nothing more attractive to offer you than Sonia and Victoire? Pah! They'd have kept!"

"You mean to say...?" whispered M. Dudouis, at last, understanding the chief-inspector's agitation.

"You've guessed it, chief!"

"Is he here?"

"He's here."

"In hiding?"

"Not a bit of it. Simply in disguise. He's the manservant."

This time, M. Dudouis did not utter a word nor make a gesture. Lupin's audacity confounded him.

Ganimard chuckled.

"It's no longer a threefold, but a fourfold incarnation. Edith Swan-neck might have blundered. The master's presence was necessary; and he had the cheek to return. For three weeks, he has been beside me during my inquiry, calmly following the progress made."

"Did you recognize him?"

"One doesn't recognize him. He has a knack of making-up his face and altering the proportions of his body so as to prevent anyone from knowing him. Besides, I was miles from suspecting.... But, this evening, as I was watching Sonia in the shadow of the stairs, I heard Victoire speak to the manservant and call him, 'Dearie.' A light flashed in upon me. 'Dearie!' That was what she always used to call him. And I knew where I was."

M. Dudouis seemed flustered, in his turn, by the presence of the enemy, so often pursued and always so intangible:

"We've got him, this time," he said, between his teeth. "We've got him; and he can't escape us."

"No, chief, he can't: neither he nor the two women."

"Where are they?"

"Sonia and Victoire are on the second floor; Lupin is on the third."

M. Dudouis suddenly became anxious:

"Why, it was through the windows of one of those floors that the tapestries were passed when they disappeared!"

"That's so, chief."

"In that case, Lupin can get away too. The windows look out on the Rue Dufresnoy."

"Of course they do, chief; but I have taken my precautions. The moment you arrived, I sent four of our men to keep watch under the windows in the Rue Dufresnoy. They have strict instructions to shoot, if anyone appears at the windows and looks like coming down. Blank cartridges for the first shot, ball-cartridges for the next."

"Good, Ganimard! You have thought of everything. We'll wait here; and, immediately after sunrise...."

"Wait, chief? Stand on ceremony with that rascal? Bother about rules and regulations, legal hours and all that rot? And suppose he's not quite so polite to us and gives us the slip meanwhile? Suppose he plays us one of his Lupin tricks? No, no, we must have no nonsense! We've got him: let's collar him; and that without delay!"

And Ganimard, all a-quiver with indignant impatience, went out, walked across the garden and presently returned with half-a-dozen men:

"It's all right, chief. I've told them, in the Rue Dufresnoy, to get their revolvers out and aim at the windows. Come along."

These alarums and excursions had not been effected without a certain amount of noise, which was bound to be heard by the inhabitants of the house. M. Dudouis felt that his hand was forced. He made up his mind to act:

"Come on, then," he said.

The thing did not take long. The eight of them, Browning pistols in hand, went up the stairs without overmuch precaution, eager to surprise Lupin before he had time to organize his defences.

"Open the door!" roared Ganimard, rushing at the door of Mme. Sparmiento's bedroom.

A policeman smashed it in with his shoulder.

There was no one in the room; and no one in Victoire's bedroom either.

"They're all upstairs!" shouted Ganimard. "They've gone up to Lupin in his attic. Be careful now!"

All the eight ran up the third flight of stairs. To his great astonishment, Ganimard found the door of the attic open and the attic empty. And the other rooms were empty too.

"Blast them!" he cursed. "What's become of them?"

But the chief called him. M. Dudouis, who had gone down again to the second floor, noticed that one of the windows was not latched, but just pushed to:

"There," he said, to Ganimard, "that's the road they took, the road of the tapestries. I told you as much: the Rue Dufresnoy...."

"But our men would have fired on them," protested Ganimard, grinding his teeth with rage. "The street's guarded."

"They must have gone before the street was guarded."

"They were all three of them in their rooms when I rang you up, chief!"

"They must have gone while you were waiting for me in the garden."

"But why? Why? There was no reason why they should go today rather than tomorrow, or the next day, or next week, for that matter, when they had pocketed all the insurance-money!"

Yes, there was a reason; and Ganimard knew it when he saw, on the table, a letter addressed to himself and opened it and read it. The letter was worded in the style of the testimonials which we hand to people in our service who have given satisfaction:

"I, the undersigned, Arsène Lupin, gentleman-burglar, ex-colonel, ex-man-of-all-work, ex-corpse, hereby certify that the person of the name of Ganimard gave proof of the most remarkable qualities during his stay in this house. He was exemplary in his behaviour, thoroughly devoted and attentive; and, unaided by the least clue, he foiled a part of my plans and saved the insurance-companies four hundred and fifty thousand francs. I congratulate him; and I am quite willing to overlook his blunder in not anticipating that the downstairs telephone communicates with the telephone in Sonia Kritchnoff's bedroom and that, when telephoning to Mr. Chief-detective, he was at the same time telephoning to me to clear out as fast as I could. It was a pardonable slip, which must not be allowed to dim the glamour of his services nor to detract from the merits of his victory.

"Having said this, I beg him to accept the homage of my admiration and of my sincere friendship.

"ARSÈNE LUPIN"

Printed in Great Britain
by Amazon